Caroline Leslie Field

High-lights

Caroline Leslie Field

High-lights

ISBN/EAN: 9783337156480

Printed in Europe, USA, Canada, Australia, Japan

Cover: Foto ©Andreas Hilbeck / pixelio.de

More available books at **www.hansebooks.com**

HIGH–LIGHTS

To larger sight
The rim of shadow is the line of light.
T. W. PARSONS.

BOSTON AND NEW YORK
HOUGHTON, MIFFLIN AND COMPANY
The Riverside Press, Cambridge
1886

The Riverside Press, Cambridge:
Electrotyped and printed by H. O. Houghton & Co.

TO MY HUSBAND.

HIGH-LIGHTS.

CHAPTER I.

" We thus begin with the beginning."

OWEN MEREDITH.

IT was a little room, not more than twelve feet square, up in the topmost corner of a big brick building. Out from its one window you looked down into a narrow, dirty court where old orange-peelings and fragments of weather - beaten newspaper found quiet refuge, or across to another big brick building, the windows of which were so coated with dust and smoke that it was as impossible to discover what lay behind them as it is to read in certain unrevealing eyes the soul that never shines through.

The room itself was like a little oasis amid the wide, tiresome desert of mercantile life ; or like a quiet, green island around whose rocky base the waves of traffic curled and foamed and broke with a low, distant monotone more soothing than utter stillness. Its four walls were hung with framed and unframed canvases : bits of Nature, arrested by Art; stretches of meadow-land where cows were feeding; shady wood-openings where the brown earth lay cool and moist, and the rough cart-paths lost themselves among low-hanging boughs. One could almost walk on, round the painted turnings, to find what lay beyond. There were river-windings and roadside pools, soft, white winter scenes, and brilliant autumnal bits; while here and there peeped out a flower study or scene of animal life, — not pansies nor roses, nor sleek, well-kept dogs and horses; but scarlet cardinal flowers, and tangled, blossomy clematis, and little, wild, shy-footed things that never wittingly had stayed for brush to sketch them.

Yet it would hardly seem that art was here followed as a profession, for no easel was to be seen ; and that air of picturesque untidiness which invariably pervades the studio was totally lacking; while, most convincing proof of all, instead of the clear, cold light that artists love, there poured in through the open window a flood of June sunshine, tempered by the soft June breeze that gently stirred the painted paper shade.

In one corner of the room a small study-table was covered with books and papers; in another a round light-stand held a huge china punch-bowl heaped with wild-flowers; out from a third opened a narrow door-way into what was evidently a bed-room beyond; and in the fourth stood a violin case. Two curiously carved chairs of English oak completed the simple furnishing.

Across one of these latter was thrown, carelessly, a gentleman's coat. Across the other was thrown, almost as carelessly, the gentleman himself. That he was a gentleman was evident at first sight, notwithstanding the shirt-sleeves and lounging posture; and when once that has been said there really seems little more to add, unless it be to note the color of his eyes, which was gray; or of his hair, which was brown; or to reckon up the years of his life and give them in round numbers as — nine and twenty, say.

Sundry articles on the floor beside him, such as a water-proof coat, wrong side out and compactly folded; an open, freshly stocked color-case with supply of brushes near by; an immaculate linen blouse whose multifarious pockets were portly with unseen deposits; and various minor articles, among which strayed, conspicuous and snake-like, a stout buff-leather shawl-strap, indicated previous exertion; while the close proximity of a shiny new Railway Guide, with a black locomotive steaming briskly into space on its yellow cover, seemed to point unmistakably to an impending start of some sort.

Meantime the man who was to make the start sat leisurely consulting his note-book, adding to or subtracting from its penciled memoranda here and there as the case might be. And his face, seen thus in repose, wore the grave, steadfast, almost stern look of a man who has his own way to make in the world, and means to make it.

As he jotted down the last entry and closed the book, there came a sound of quick, springing steps over the stairs without, and another, much younger man appeared in the door-way. With the bright smile of greeting which Conrad Faulkner flashed upon his friend, every trace of sternness was swept away, and the firm lips grew strangely sweet.

"Just in time, Terry! I must be off in an hour. Sit down, if you can find anything to sit on, while I write a few lines to Hegemann."

Terry, otherwise Chester Jackson, drew forward the other chair, tossing the gray coat unceremoniously down on the before-mentioned pile at his feet; and, seating himself astride its faded crimson cushion, rested his folded arms, with his chin upon them, across the carved back and proceeded to wait, quietly, until the other should have done.

The two faces thus opposed to each other, though both pleasant and goodly to behold, were very different. That of the new-comer, while it lacked the firm maturity of his companion's, yet had a charm, all its own, in the fresh look of frank boyishness which, from the laughing dark-blue eyes to the smoothly rounded chin, was its pervading characteristic. And the other, though gifted less, perhaps, with positive beauty, bore, stamped clearly and unmistakably upon its every feature, that look which is so far beyond any mere accident of form or coloring, — the look of a man who lives from high motives, worthily. The one was a youthful David, going forth light-hearted and confident — perhaps the merest trifle over-confident — to do battle with that tough old Goliath, the World. The other, a strong, calm Michael, already wrestling in the thick of the fight, but borne up by those two mighty wings of which Thomas à Kempis tells us, and beating down Satan under his feet.

Among their mutual acquaintances it was considered rather a queer thing that these two should be such close friends. One, a man near thirty, traveled, well-read, a writer himself of reviews and leading articles for prominent periodicals; already rising by his own merit and exertion to a front place in literary ranks; giving himself no leisure and but little rest save as he fled, now and then, for a couple of months to the wilderness, with his paint-pots and brushes, to be lazy in the way he liked best. The other, a boy of twenty-three, barely out of college, with no discernible ambition beyond having a good time, and spending his snug little income (of which the principal was safely tied up, under the control of his grandfather for two years to come: Master Terry mean time being bound. whether he liked or no, to serve in the capacity of clerk in the former's counting-room) "like a gentleman."

Perhaps it was because of just this total unlikeness, each finding his complement in the other; perhaps it was because their first meeting, two years before, had been in the dreary parlor of a little out-of-the-way German inn, where the face of a fellow-countryman was like a star in a cloudy night; or perhaps it was because of something lying latent under all Terry's youth and nonsense that other people were too obtuse to discover. Be that as it may, the friendship stood, and came to be cause and revealer of much, both in lives and characters, that might otherwise have lain dormant or never come to pass.

The brief note was soon written and sealed, and Conrad Faulkner turned once more to his friend.

"Well, Terry, my boy, what luck? does the old gentleman relent at all?"

"Relent?" echoed the other, morosely, "not he. Catch him relenting! I put my foot down, too, though, this morning. He can't cheat me out of my vacation entirely. I told him I should go when Harding got back, anyhow."

" What did he say to that respectful announcement ? "

" Growled fearfully. And old Crabbe vowed he 'd send for me if business picked up. Business won't pick up, though, and I can stand the growling. But I 've got to wait till July."

" All right. Then we 'll wait. I can take a run down into Maine, and meet you in Boston later."

" No, you can't. Read that ! "

" That " was a letter which Terry drew from his breast-pocket and threw across to Conrad, who was now down on his knees engaged in a desperate struggle with the buff-leather shawl-strap aforesaid, which had turned obstinate at the last moment, as such unreasoning things ·will, and refused to give way so far as to buckle where it was wanted to do.

" In a minute. Just toss me that penknife, will you ? I must make a new hole here."

This being done, and the contrary strap fastened securely, the victor seated himself upon his prostrate foe, and picking up the envelope proceeded to make himself acquainted with its contents.

Highfield Farm, Ockley, N. H.,
June 6, 18—.

DEAR NEPHEW TERRY, — It is a disappointment to both Robina and myself that you cannot visit us at present. Doubtless, however, your grandfather has his reasons — and good ones — for requesting you to postpone it. A man in his responsible position must drive carefully. Business is a clumsy vehicle, and the wheels will not run under. But even if you must wait till next month, why cannot Mr. Faulkner come, as agreed? Since learning from Classmate Green that he is the son of my old friend Dick Faulkner, I have experienced a great desire to meet and talk with him ; and earnestly wish that he would consent to waive all ceremony, and come up at once. ·Robina and I are not gay people exactly, but Ockley in itself will go far with a man of his tastes ; and for the rest — we will try to keep him content until you arrive at least.

Urge this matter, my boy, and tell Mr. F——, with my best regard, that we shall depend upon seeing him at the time originally fixed.

Affectionately yours,
ISAAC N. CARY.

"Well?" interrogated Terry, just a bit impatiently.

"Well," repeated Conrad, slowly.

"What do you say? I 'm to 'urge,' you know. Just consider yourself urged, will you? and give a fellow your decision. Say yes and be done with it!"

"That is easy. Easier than it would be to say no. One could not well refuse such an invitation, even if one wanted to, which I do not. You 're a lucky dog, Terry, to have two such homes. Some people would be thankful for one."

"Some people are n't, Con Faulkner, then, for he 's the hardest-mouthed mule where sociability is concerned that ever I tried to drive. "You know, Con," he added, gravely, for his friend's homelessness always touched a tender spot in his boy heart, "you know I am always ready to go shares with you in everything; but you 'll never budge."

"I 'm budging now with a vengeance, if only I don't 'live to regret it.' That used to be my Aunt Hetty's favorite threat whenever I ventured to indulge in a youthful lark. 'You 'll live to regret it, child!' And to tell the truth I have lived to regret most of the times when I have ventured to crawl out into other people's sunshine for a bit. The crawling back is not so pleasant. Nothing deepens the shadows in a picture like throwing out a few high-lights."

" Are n't you rather putting the cart before the horse, old man? I always thought you painters threw out your lights by deepening the shadows."

" That's the lingo, certainly, and it's a poor rule that does n't work both ways ; but you must have your light first, or you may whistle for your shade."

" Moral — take care not to stand in your own light if you don't want to see shadows. You 're on the right tack this time, Con ; it's all ' high - lights ' at Ockley. Confound it all though ! " he exclaimed, waxing wrathful again over his wrongs ; " it's shady lines for me. I never intended getting left when I planned the business, all so fine ! "

" Assuredly I never intended you should when I agreed to it," laughed his friend. " Cheer up, Terry ! July is bound to come, and Miss Robina will be doubly glad to see you after a surfeit of your humble servant and his traps. Elderly ladies don't usually take kindly to having their spare room littered up with truck of this sort." And he

indicated the surrounding art collection with
a sweep of his arm.

Terry's eyes flashed and twinkled.

"Cousin Rob — ina is not to say elderly,
exactly. I guess you never heard me say
very much about her, Con."

"Very little beyond the fact that she keeps
house for your uncle and is Lady Bountiful
to the parish at large. A whole - souled,
motherly sort of person, I take it, with a
decided leaning toward her graceless young
cousin."

Terry grinned.

"Well, Con, if those are your precon-
ceived notions, it would be a pity to spoil
them, so I 'll say nothing. Only — if she
does n't prove quite as 'motherly' as you
expect, don't blame me."

"No, I 'll praise you. That will be the
surest way to get into her good graces. It
will take all your virtues to cloak my sins."

"I 'm not so sure of that as I wish I
were," murmured Terry to the chair-back.
But he hastened to add, with a mischievous
glance at Conrad, "Praise up the gray cat
and the pot-pie if you want to make yourself popular. Uncle Ike's housekeeper is
a tip-top cook."

"An excellent thing in woman. What's the time, Terry? I must hurry."

"Quarter to four, by Jove! Some one else must hurry too, I reckon, or be late to dinner. Good-by, old man. You hang on there till July, and I'll be on hand — Providence and old Crabbe permitting. I'll write the Dominie to - night and tell him your're coming. Take care of yourself, Con, and leave the keys with Rooney, will you? I like to run in sometimes, though the place seems like an old tomb when I'm alone in it."

The merry face was grave, and the grave face smiling as the two friends grasped each other's hands. Yet somehow the smile held as much of regret as the gravity.

Two days later Conrad Faulkner was mounting the stairs of a down-town Boston building, the front of which fairly bristled with wooden signs and lacquered tin strips innumerable. Two long flights were traversed rapidly and without hesitation ; at the foot of the third he paused, thought a moment, turned sharp to the left, and walked along the narrow corridor to a door at the extreme end which bore upon its brass plate the inscription —

BENJAMIN THACHER

COUNSELLOR AT LAW.

A deep voice called "Come in!" in answer to his knock; but before he could turn the knob the door flew back on its hinges, and a sturdy little old gentleman with a gray head sprang out, like a Jack-in-the-box, and seizing the young man in his arms hugged him with a vehemence that would have done credit to a brown bear.

"Thought 't was your knock, boy. Come in — come in! there's your chair waiting for you. Got telegram, all right, at eleven. Mighty glad to get it too. Bless my stars, you're just the same old sixpence! Put your traps down in the corner. I'll be ready in twenty minutes, and then we'll go home to dinner. I've corn four inches high already, and you never tasted such lettuce and peas as I can give you in your life! Now make yourself comfortable, and don't speak a word to me till I get out of this snarl."

Conrad laughed and obeyed; while he of the gray head plunged deep into the contents of various papers and documents on the table before him.

Promptly at the time designated, however, he emerged; reduced chaos to order with quick and practised hand; and, catching up hat and driving-gloves, announced himself ready to start.

"You see, Con," said he, as they descended the stairs and stepped out into the street, "there's nothing like farming for the fun of the thing. Turn down here; I stable at Herrick's now; he's nearer than Blake, besides being a good deal more reliable. These farmers who have to make their living off their land are so terribly afraid of experiments! Now I've four dozen as pretty hills of corn as ever you saw; four inches high; and no one else about here has it much more than planted. How do you think I did it? Started it under glass. The neighbors all laugh and shake their heads over it, and I suppose it does look rather crazy to men who plant their sweet corn by the acre; but I shall have it in the pot before theirs begins to ear, for all that. Here we are. Always on hand, Jerry — hey? Jump in, Con! all right; now give 'em their heads!" and the two gentlemen, bowing their own as they passed under the low doorway, drove up the street at a pace which might have proved dangerous with any less skillful hand on the reins than "Old Ben Thacher's."

Once fairly free from city obstructions, the lawyer's steady attention to his horses relaxed somewhat, and conversation went on unflaggingly ; owing chiefly, it must be confessed, to the cheery garrulity of the elder man, who was evidently heartily attached to his newly arrived guest.

"Well, well, well!" he exclaimed at length, "how much talking it takes to sew up a two years gap. Back and forth, back and forth, like Constance's thread when she is darning stockings. It 'll take a week at least to cobble up this hole. And yet, I declare, it does n't seem as long as that since we were thumping about together on those hard-backed Swiss horses, and not much longer since you and I were pulling Connie through that terrible siege at Rome. She never would have come through either but for you, boy. Hem! get along, Polka! we must n't be late to dinner. The old lady will be on tiptoe. I sent your telegram out to her by Ferris. Knew she 'd never forgive me if she had n't a chance to kill the fatted calf and get on her best cap. Whey, Mazurka!"

The sun was shooting golden arrows between the trunks of stalwart elms that lined each side of the way, as the well-matched roans trotted easily along the broad, level stretch of Winford Street. It flashed keenly across the faces of the two men in the buggy while a short, unsheltered strip of dusty road was traversed, and subsided again to a mere twinkle through drooping boughs and thickly interlacing vines as a corner was turned into a long shaded avenue, which, after taking several turns itself between its green borderings of birches and cat-brier and wild grape-vines, took a last one, and brought up before the broad, low veranda of a broad, low house.

Miss Constance Thacher, a sweet-faced lady of some sixty years, housekeeper, adviser, and dearest friend to her warm-hearted, impetuous old-bachelor brother, met them, with a glad welcome for Conrad, in the hall, and the three were presently seated at table in the cool dining-room; through the long, open windows of which they could watch the river winding its shining length between green, shelving banks, the red and white cows browsing their leisurely way home from pasture, and, further off, the creeping ranges of low-lying hills, with a June sun sinking slowly in golden glory beyond them all.

"There, now!" exclaimed Mr. Thacher, when, peas and lettuce having been duly attended to and commended, hot meats and puddings sent away, and the cloth removed, the trio sat cosily in the gathering twilight over their fruit; "this is just as it should be. All three together again. Honestly, now, Conrad, does it seem as if it were two years since you left us at the Liverpool dock, and set that obstinate face of yours toward making your own way in the world?"

"Honestly, I should say it seemed more like six, sir. Years are very much like that worn-out old shield in the reading-book; whether they seem short or long, dark or bright, depends upon a person's stand-point. I have been on the shady side of so many lately that I hardly remember how the reverse looks. I 've broken loose this summer to try to find out."

"All right; we 'll help you. Connie and I. How do you propose to begin?"

"It strikes me I have made a fairly good beginning already."

"Well, then, how do you mean to keep on?"

"As I have begun, for a time. Then I am due at Ockley, as I told you. Terry will join me in July, and then we propose to scour the surrounding country on foot; always keeping his uncle's house as head-quarters, however, for Terry has sat in the lap of luxury too long to appreciate the joys of up-country taverns. You should know Terry," he continued, turning to Miss Constance; "he is just one of the generous, merry-hearted boys such as you like. There is the making of a very noble man in him too, if I am not mistaken."

"He is n't the sort of boy I like," broke in Mr. Thacher; "interferes too much with my plans. So does the old chum up in the back-woods, who, by the way, seems to have raked up his college recollections rather late in the day. However, he 'll do to drop. Con, Sis and I have arranged to take a couple of weeks off, or rather to take ourselves off for that length of time, somewhere about the end of August or first of September. Every dog has his day about that time, and I 'm bound to have mine. A man gets tired of his own vine and fig-tree once in a while, especially if he never gets a chance to sit under it, and I 've been pretty hard worked ever since we came back from Europe. Connie's heart is set on it too, and it does n't agree with the Thacher constitution to be disappointed. But we can't go without you, so when will you be ready? Name the day, and I 'll choke off my clients to suit."

" To tell the truth," said Conrad, " I hardly see how I can manage it, much as I should like to do so. I had intended to be back in New York again by September 1st at latest."

" But, man alive, you promised us a visit. You don't intend to break your word, do you ? "

" It does n't look much like it, at present," replied Conrad, smiling, " since I am here to redeem it. I can give you a couple of weeks now, unless Miss Constance would rather I made it one."

" Well, upon my word ! " Mr. Thacher fairly dropped the strawberry that was half-way to his mouth back upon the plate, and flung down his spoon in disgust. " All the time he wants for old Daddy Cary, and two paltry little weeks for us ! I guess you forget that if Providence had n't seen fit to interfere I might have been your uncle."

" No, I don't," said Conrad ; but his excited host sandwiched this remark without even noticing it.

" It 's all very well for the Bible to enjoin hospitality, and I trust and believe I do my best to bear out St. Peter under all circumstances ; but the guest has some responsibility in the matter, I take it ; and, if you can call yourself a hospitable man, Con Faulkner, in the face of such a speech as that you just made, your conscience must be tough for your years, — re-markably tough ! "

"Never mind, Ben," put in his sister, laughing, " you just go on doing as the Bible tells you to, and leave the boy to me. I 'll manage him. Ben is quite right, Conrad," she added, " if he is rather rude about it ; and moreover " —

" Rude ? I 'm not rude," interrupted Mr. Thacher, nodding his head emphatically. " I 'm merely extending a pressing invitation. It 's not all politeness, either ; it 's part business. I want you to paint a picture of old Victory. Well, what are you humping up your eyebrows at now ? "

" I fear the result would be a picture of defeat," replied the young man, bringing down the too-expressive eyebrows.

" De-fiddle-sticks, boy! No such thing. I know what I 'm about. Victory is n't one of your sleek, pink-nosed, crook-neck snorters! He 's a rough and tough old fellow, with character in his face. That horse has had a history, and he knows it. I want some one to paint him who will catch his expression. You 're a great one for catching expressions, Con."

" My dear Ben! I hope he won't catch any of yours."

" Don't you bother, Connie," said the lawyer, with a quick smile at his sister that robbed the words of all roughness. " The boy understands me and my ways. Come, young man," turning again to Conrad, " what do you say; will you or won't you? "

" It would be only a pleasure to make the attempt so far as I 'm concerned," replied his guest, " but I fear you would hardly feel proud of the result. Victory is a grand old fellow, a regular Lear among horses; he deserves to be painted by a master-hand. Why not get Lawshe to do it? I never painted a horse in my life."

" Neither did Lawshe, for that matter." Miss Constance exclaimed.

" Oh, I know he has had some four-legged

things on exhibition ; perhaps he calls them horses. I don't. They 're mere daubs — animated daubs! not like any horse that ever was seen, unless it may be a night-mare ! "

" Perhaps your opinion would not be worth much in art circles, Ben," suggested his sister.

" May be not. I guess it would n't, seeing that Lawshe's is. I know what I like, though, and that 's more than half these critics do. Regular hypocrites, most of 'em ! Turning their conceited backs on what really takes one's fancy, and squinting through their fingers at things that are enough to give one the crawls to look at, merely because they are considered the correct thing. By and by some other style will be considered the correct thing, and then these modern fellows will be worse off than the old ones are now; for they, at least, did their best to paint things as they saw them; whereas these chaps are forever straining themselves to paint things as a certain set of ' non - compusses ' wants to see them ! "

" Don't talk so loud, Ben, please."

" And then," went on Mr. Thacher, after a glance at his sister, in a mild tone which, taken in connection with his excited face and gestures, was inconceivably comical, — " then they find fault with such pictures as Hilton's because of their ' finish.' Finish! I tell you if you 're going to imitate the Lord's handiwork you 've got to finish. I would n't give that bull of Hilton's that hangs in my office for all the hysterics these folks can put on canvas. Good gracious, man, any one can throw paint! I could do it myself. Look at that picture that Farley bought; how did the man do it? I 'll tell you. He just slapped the canvas with a red paint-brush, wiped it with a brown one, tickled it a little with palette scrapings, hung it up ten yards off, and called it 'Foxes'! And then Farley goes and pays five hundred dollars for it — like a fool. Foxes! why a fox would turn gray at the sight of it. But just look at that bull, now! he 's got hairs. You won't find any streaks on him. Put the breath of life into him, and he 'd bellow at you with a will. Those confounded foxes would blow up if they tried to breathe."

" I 'm afraid you will blow up if you don't, Ben."

" Well, well," said he, good-humoredly,

mopping his face with his napkin, and emerging very rubicund and glossy. " Hang art, anyhow! Nature's the thing for me. Come along and see my corn, Con, before it gets too dark."

They quitted the table at that, and the two gentlemen went out together to stroll for a while among the flowers and vegetables which were the pride of the lawyer's heart; while Miss Constance sat in the gathering dusk, on the wide piazza, clicking her shining knitting-needles softly against each other, and watching the moon as it rose buoyantly up into the fathomless blue.

Presently Conrad came back alone, and seated himself on the step at her feet.

" This is a glorious night! " said he.

" June nights are apt to be glorious. And especially so among the hills. I am right glad you are to have a breath of mountain air again, Conrad. It is what you need. You look thinner and older than when we parted in England."

" I am older by two pretty hard years."

" Not too old to grow young again if you have the chance. That is why I want you to take it now, before the lines and wrinkles become chronic. Going among pleasant people will tend to smooth them out wonderfully."

"To tell the truth I rather dread that part of it. I believe I do not make friends easily."

"My dear, friends are not like doughnuts, to be twisted together out of common material by the aid of a little sugar and spice. The Lord gives them to us as he sees we need them. Only — when they come, hold on to them."

The busy needles traveled to and fro along the edge of the white cloud of yarn. Neither the lady nor the gentleman spoke again for some minutes. He was enjoying, with all his artist's heart, the effect of the soft, clear moonlight, that made a fairy vision of the wide lawn, with its clumps of shrubbery and grand old trees. She was revolving in her mind something which pressed for utterance, yet found no words quite fitting. Presently she grew desperate, and spoke the first that offered.

"Conrad, dear boy, I have a feeling somehow in my bones that this summer will be a turning-point for you."

"Yes? I suppose every moment is a turning-point if one only knew it. Do you notice how exquisite those shadows of the grape-vines are upon the boles of the white birches yonder?"

"Very, very lovely indeed. But only shadows after all. Do you know I think you have kept companionship with shadows long enough. I am very glad that some one is trying to drag you out into the sunshine for a while."

"'Out among the high-lights,' as Terry says," replied he, smiling.

"Precisely. I want to know this Terry presently. Bring him with you — if he will come when you come back in September. For of course, Conrad," she went on, quickly, looking down at him with earnest eyes, "you will come back to us. If we let you break away from us after that year in Europe, which by its deep experiences did the work of twenty ordinary years in linking our lives together, it was only because your own highest good demanded that your life-plan should be your own, and worked out by yourself. Where mother and father would not interfere, it was not for us to do so; but, wherever and whenever mother or father could welcome or advise or help, we claim it as our right to do so, Ben and I.

Go out into the world as you will ; but, when the times for home - coming offer, this is home.   Will you remember?"

Conrad sprang to his feet. "I am not likely to forget," he said, in a low, intense tone, as he paced the bright veranda with folded arms, "either the words you have now spoken or the many others of wonderful kindness which have been said before.   It is not that I am ungrateful for your goodness that I hesitate to avail myself of it more," he went on, pausing in his earnestness beside Miss Constance ; "you must believe that! It is only that, when one has got used to living among shadows, too much of the other thing — dazzles one's eyes!"   And either because his eyes were dazzled, or for some other reason, he walked off to the far end of the veranda with quick strides.

Miss Constance took advantage of this movement to polish up her glasses and wipe her own eyes. Then she remarked, quietly, —

"Of course it was to be expected that these two years would be rather dreary, among strangers as you were, with Ben and me away, and the old place shut up.   But now that is all set right, and even if you were in Kamschatka it would not seem so bad, since home is here for you to come to when you need it. I am so glad, too, my dear, that you are to be in New York. Chicago always seemed a chain-lightning sort of place to me. And you will find it as easy to run on for Thanksgiving and Christmas as you used to find it to run over here for comfort and gingerbread, when Aunt Hetty was particularly rigorous, poor soul!"

"'Rigorous' is a good word," laughed Conrad, coming back to his old seat on the steps. "Aunt Hetty was all that. She thought she was merely doing her duty, I suppose."

"That is what comes of living all alone," exclaimed Miss Constance. "I would rather adopt a poor-house. It spoils a woman or a man, either. I shall be so glad"—full stop.

"Of what?" he asked, turning to her with the sudden smile that sometimes lit his grave face into most winning beauty.

Miss Constance made a sidewise dive for her ball.

"I shall be so glad—to see you happily married. Mrs. Conrad will be a great comfort to me in more ways than one."

The grave look crept back again, and

there was silence while Miss Constance knitted six stitches, dropping intermediate ones promiscuously. Then Conrad spoke, quietly.

"I have never met her yet. I sometimes think I never shall."

"Yes you will," asserted Miss Constance, stoutly. "And when you do, Conrad, don't do as I did. I waited. Don't you wait. Marry!"

"Marry? who talks of marrying?" exclaimed a gruff voice from the darkness of the deserted room within. "Constance Thacher, what do you mean by putting such notions into our boy's head? We can't spare him yet a while, and the dickens only knows how much we should see of him if he had a wife!"

"No danger at present," laughed the "boy." "I can't afford such luxuries."

"Hah! don't know about that, either," retorted his host. "These summer vacations are dangerous things, especially to knights of the pen and the paint-pot. When Art meets Nature then comes the tug-of-war. I expect nothing but that you'll get snapped up by some blowsy country-girl."

There was a general laugh at this prophetic outburst, and then Mr. Thacher and Conrad fell to talking of horses and crops and the desirability of being in two places at once when circumstances required it; while Miss Constance put in a quiet word here and there, or, busily flashing back the moonbeams from her four restless little rods of steel, looked far out into the mysterious shadowy region of things to come, and smiled to herself over her own unspoken fancies.

CHAPTER II.

THE midday rays of a summer sun were pouring hotly down upon the wide, bare platform at Cutter's Falls. The still heat radiated from the steep, rocky sides of the surrounding hills, till the little basin, of which the great brick depot occupied the centre, fairly rippled and waved with visible caloric. Nothing was moving but two dusty, forlorn looking hens. Nothing was audible save the faint, monotonous click-click which issued from behind the closed blinds of the telegraph office. The hot hands of the big depot clock moved slowly round till they pointed to twenty minutes of twelve. Nothing stirred. Fifteen minutes of twelve — a brisk step sounded, and the station-master appeared, coming round the corner of the building.

Ten minutes — there came a rattle of wheels and tramping of horses as the hotel stages drove alongside the platform, wheeled, backed up, and waited; the drivers lying lazily along the tops of their vehicles, with reins held loosely in one hand.

Five minutes of the hour. The old flag-man shuffled along, with his red signal, and took up his position at the crossing.

Suddenly the great steam-whistle on the factory by the bridge drew up its black, iron palate, and sent forth from its metallic throat a ringing scream that was flung back, in deafening clangor, from every rock and tree until, as the last echo died away among the quiet hills, there came an answering scream from the woods beyond the river; and, hot and dusty from its rush of a hundred miles, the noon train from Boston rounded with slackening speed the shining curve of rail, and drew up slowly, panting, before the station.

In an instant the place was all alive. Streams of passengers emptied themselves from the various cars, until, across the space but a moment before empty and deserted, it was hard to find a pathway. Trunks and boxes whirled through the air in a manner agonizing to the anxious eyes of their owners. Draymen shouted and hauled.

The lazy stage-drivers, alert and active now, plucked women by the sleeve and men by the coat-tail, vociferously shouting out the superior merits and advantages of their respective hotels; while a stout, red - faced man in a white apron brandished a big bell over the heads of the bewildered multitude — its resonant tongue hardly more clamorous than his own — as he assured the " ladies and gentlemen " that they would have " twenty minutes for dinner ! "

Conrad Faulkner, alighting with the crowd, made the best of his way out of it, and the unsheltered glare at the front, into comparative isolation and a cooler spot at the rear of the building. In one corner of an unoccupied settee he deposited his hand-bag and a stalky-looking bundle consisting of umbrella, camp-stool, etc. ; looked about for a small boy to act as guardian of his treasures ; but descrying none concluded to trust to Providence and the traditional honesty of country towns for a few minutes, and plunged once more, Orpheus-like, into the Inferno he had just left, searching for his Eurydice, — a small russet trunk with C. F. in black letters on either end.

Having found and rescued it, the next

desideratum was a means of conveyance.
He therefore accosted a man who seemed
likely to fall an easy prey to Satanic influence, — having remained calmly in one spot,
with hands in his pockets, " unmoved by
the rush of the throng," ever since the train
came in, — and demanded of him where the
Oakley stage was to be found.

Apparently the man was unused to such
rapid utterance ; for he looked surprised,
and remained silent some seconds longer.
Then, slowly withdrawing one hand from
its place of concealment, he indicated with
its thumb an indefinite locality over his
shoulder, and replied, oracularly, " The man
that drives it's in there," — and immediately relapsed, more completely than ever,
into silence — and his pockets.

At this moment the questioner's eye, and
almost his breath, was arrested by an ap-
parition which issued from the main door of
the depot. It was, or looked to be, a boy
of about sixteen ; evidently not possessed of
his full share of wits, yet with a certain
shrewd, good - natured twinkle about the
small, pig-like eyes set deep in a round expanse of fat face, from which a freckled
snub-nose emerged like a rock in the ocean.

His hands and feet were rather small, and
his body was immense ; which imparted to
his gait a peculiar effect — something between a roll and a shuffle.

"Dickens's fat boy, by George!" ejaculated Faulkner.

"No he ain't," volunteered his indolent
acquaintance, "he 's Burns's boy; an' he 's
the very feller ye want.   Hullo, Cy!"

The fat boy turned in their direction, and
the pig's eyes twinkled.

"This man wants ter be took over to
Ockley.   Where 's Hebray?"

Conrad, unable to remove his fascinated
gaze from the boy, beheld a sudden con-
tortion of countenance which twisted the
mouth round almost to the left ear, but
heard no sound issue from the lips.   Instead
there seemed to come from some one just
behind him, in a high, squeaky voice, these
words, —

"He 's loadin' up naow; ye 'd better step
lively!"

Involuntarily he looked over his shoulder.
The indolent man laughed.

"Pretty well done, Cy!   He 's dreadful
spry with his voice" he added, in an aside
to Faulkner.   "I 've knowed him throw it

as fur as from here ter them woods yander.
He 'll do it ag'in in a minute, an' 't ain't no
sort o' use ter git used to 't — he 'll fool ye
sure, every time."

Cy, however, having manifested his vocal
powers to his own and the stranger's satisfaction, betrayed no disposition to repeat
the performance ; but shouldered the russet
trunk, with wonderful agility for one of his
build, and moved off, its owner following,
to where, close by the settee on which reposed the other articles just as they had
been left, stood now an antiquated yellow
and black stage-coach drawn by two bony
old bays ; while an equally bony and ma-
hogany - colored driver, with innumerable
wrinkles in his face and a pair of gold ear-
rings in his ears, was busying himself with
various barrels and packages on the rack
behind.

Having seen his belongings made fast with
the rest, Conrad mounted the top-heavy old
trap, which accommodatingly bent itself to
meet him as it felt his weight upon the step,
thereby causing an unexpected strain upon
the muscles of the back and abdomen anything but agreeable. It required some care
and skill to keep his balance, but he finally

succeeded in effecting this nice adjustment, and was fast losing himself in admiration of the lights and shades and exquisitely blended tints upon the mountain side before him, when suddenly the earth seemed to give way beneath him ! he felt himself jerked through space, so to speak ; and, clutching at a leather strap for safety, turned to behold the primary cause of it all.

An exceedingly solid lady, in a great green calash, from whose depths two owl-like eyes glared out upon him through gold-bowed spectacles, had essayed to mount un-aided ; and, with one foot on the step and both hands grasping the uprights, gallantly maintained her position in the face of fate, all undaunted by the fact that the back of her head threatened to strike the ground beneath her, and that a well-grown young man, with various bundles, was in imminent danger of being precipitated upon her from above.

Conrad bit his lip violently to force down his emotions ; and, keeping tight hold of the strap with one hand, offered the other to his helpless vis-à-vis.

" That 's right, young man ! jest you hang holt there, like grim death to a dead nigger, an' I 'll git right in." And, suiting the action to the words, she grasped the proffered hand tightly in her own big, freckled one, and, with much puffing and effort and a lavish display of garter, hoisted herself triumphantly to a seat in the elastic chariot.

"There! I 'm obleeged to ye, I declare. Hebray, he 's ginerally on hand ter boost, but seems he warn't this time. Sorry ter upsot your equalibberum so."

"Not at all, Madam," replied Conrad, with well-recovered gravity; "my equilibrium is not easily upset, although I must confess the experience of the past few moments has been quite a strain upon it."

"Should n't wonder if it hed. More ways 'n one, mebbe!" retorted his companion, with a shrewd twinkle in the eyes behind the spectacles. "Laff all ye want ter, I don't mind. 'T was funny, an' no mistake!" And she fairly led off the laugh herself, her broad shoulders shaking with jolly appreciation of the joke.

"Be you a-goin' ter Ockley ter *stop?*" she inquired further, after a pause.

"For a time, yes."

"Ruther guess you 're the man they 've be'n expectin' up to Parson Cary's this three fo' days, ain't ye?"

" Very likely.   I am going there."

" Us two 'll meet ag'in then, as the song says.   I belong up that way too.   Say ! " she called to the driver, who now appeared escorting two more female passengers and a band-box, " ye may set me down ter Mary Jane's.   Seth 'll tackle up 'n take me hum by 'n by."

He of the gold ear-rings nodded and spat ; and, having established his charges on the back seat by dint of two vigorous " boosts " such as the stout lady had spoken of, extended an invitation to Conrad to share the front seat with himself ; which change of base being effected, he clucked to his steeds, and the procession moved.

For eight miles the road from Cutter's Falls to Ockley lay through a thickly wooded valley — an easy stretch for the gaunt horses, who traveled steadily on except for occasional stops to deliver bags of potatoes and barrels of flour by the way, and a rather prolonged halt at Mary Jane's.

The driver, whose name appeared in black lettering on the yellow coach-body as Z. Hebray, proved to be of a loquacious turn, and conversed amicably with his only male passenger in a voice which alternated between a raucous growl and a subdued wheeze, as his bronchitis or his asthma got the upper hand. The fat boy had disappeared.

"There's Mill Village meetin' 'us," quoth Mr. Hebray, after some hour and a half of steady jogging, pointing with the butt of his whip to a church-spire rising white from out a nest of green. "And the hotel's close by. Shall I drop ye there, Mister, or do ye want ter be kerried sumw'er's? I've got ter leave these wimmen round fust, that's inside here, an' then I'll take ye anyw'er's — in reason."

"Mister" thanked him, but feeling strongly moved in favor of renovation and dinner, after his long ride and longer fast, before presenting himself to people whom he had never seen, signified his perfect readiness to be "dropped," and was accordingly deposited with his traps on the bare hotel piazza; discovering Cy, as the stage rumbled off, seated in ponderous solitude on the now empty rack, his legs dangling as if forgotten by their owner, and his big straw hat tipped low over his eyes.

Two hours later, rested and refreshed, Conrad sought the landlord, paid his bill, and inquired the way to Highfield Farm.

" Never hearn on't," was the reply.

This was unexpected discouragement. Conrad tried again.

" Where does Mr. Cary, the minister, live ? "

" Want ter know ef that's what ye call *his* place ! "

" That is what he himself calls it, I believe."

" Well, there ain't another man in town that doos, then.   We all call it Saints' Rest. I donno 'baout no Highfield Fa'm, but Saints' Rest is two an' a ha'f mile from here, goin' that way."   And he pointed with a stubby finger.   Conrad thanked him, and was turning away.   The landlord called after him.

" 'Ts a braownish haouse, sits up high ! looks as much like a good-sized corn ba'n 's anything else.   Ye can't mistake it.   Two mile from here, a straight road ! Leastways," he explained to himself, watching the tall, manly figure that was already almost out of hearing, " 't ain't very straight, but there ain't no other."

Straight it certainly was not, for it turned and twisted till even Conrad, used as he was to finding his way through strange places, fairly lost his bearings, and could not, for

the life of him, tell which of the two church-
spires he saw off at the right, brought near
together by distance, belonged to the little
village he had just left. After a while, however, this whimsical road seemed to grow
tired of running away after every little rise of
ground merely for the pleasure of running
round it, and began to go straight — up!
The last mile was one continual climb. Now
along a bit of shady space where the trees
on either side the narrow way bent over in
a green and leafy screen-work; now over a
hot, unsheltered strip which must be traversed to reach the cool and tempting stretch
beyond. At one point a hurrying brook
rushed, as if out of breath with running,
under a rude board bridge; and, in sheer
despair of ever reaching its destination on
time, flung itself, with reckless haste, down
thirty feet over the sharp gray rocks that
stung it into indignant, sparkling foam.

"Ockley begins well," thought Conrad, as
he paused for a moment's breath, and enjoyment of the extended outlook, before
tackling the last steep ascent, on whose brow
he saw, perched like a big brown bird, the
house which, as the landlord had told him,
was not to be mistaken in its total unlike-

ness to all the variety of red, white, and black farm-houses scattered about over the surrounding hills.

"Saints' Rest." Truly the place seemed fair and peaceful enough for any saint to rest in; for any sinner to forget his sins and begin anew in. To Conrad Faulkner, being no saint, neither the blackest kind of sinner, it seemed, when he passed through the little rustic gate and closed it noiselessly behind him as if the whole pack of wants and disappointments which a life of nearly thirty years had laid upon his metaphorical shoulders loosed its grip, and went rolling down the hill as Christian's did. And, truly, if the hill of old had been but half as steep and toilsome an ascent as that which led to Parson Cary's cottage, the weary pilgrim might reasonably have believed that the heavy burden would never find its way up again!

The house itself was a low, Swiss-like structure, standing with open, hospitable door beneath the shadow of cool-spreading elms. A generous porch was shady with woodbine and fragrant with flowering honey-suckle; and as Conrad made his way to it along the narrow, graveled path the tones of a voice, reading, came pleasantly through the open window and mingled itself with the humming of the bees in the blossoms outside. In a moment it ceased and there was the sound of a door opening and closing. Then all was still.

"Miss Robina has departed to her kitchen," he said to himself. "I remember Aunt Hetty never could read aloud for ten consecutive minutes without jumping up to see if the muffins were rising. Now is my time!" And he lifted and let fall the heavy brass hand which did duty as a substitute for other people's knuckles.

At the sound of his knock reverberating through the quiet house, an old man with a ruddy, genial face under frosty hair came forth from the room within, and instantly advanced to greet him with ready smile and cordial, outstretched hand.

"Mr. Faulkner, I am sure! Come in, come in. You are most gladly welcome. We have been looking for you this day or two past. Bless my soul, how like you are to your father!"

He took Conrad's bag from his hand and led the way through the wide hall to the stairs.

"I am going to take you directly up to your room; and then you will start right and feel more at home, which is what I particularly want you to feel." And the old gentleman beamed upon the young one so hospitably that the latter began immediately to experience a sense of restfulness and home comfort to which he had long been a stranger.

A door at the head of the stairs stood open into a large square chamber, with four windows overlooking the valley to east and north, — the hill near whose summit Saints' Rest was built forming a kind of peninsula from which, on three sides, one looked across broad intervales to other hills beyond. All the windows were open, and the blinds had been thrown back to admit wandering breezes. The white dimity hangings of the bed and the light cane chairs and sofa seemed doubly refreshing to one who had just left city heat and dust behind; while the clean straw matting underfoot was like a revelation after weeks of dingy Brussels.

"There," said the parson, depositing the bundle of umbrellas. "This room belongs to you. The remainder of the house you must be content to take on shares with the rest of us; but this is yours, to do as you please in. Bring anything into it except a dislike for Ockley; take anything out of it except your trunk. That, I hope, will take root for some time to come. And, by the way, I must send Abijah right down for it. It's at the hotel of course? that is right. Do not hurry down if you prefer a little rest. We shall be glad to see you whenever you care to come, and we shall take tea at half past six." And the parson betook himself and his cheery smile off downstairs again.

When, some twenty minutes later, Conrad followed him, — having small desire for rest, — the first sound that greeted his ears as he opened his door was the voice of the invisible reader. "A remarkably pleasant voice for a middle-aged spinster partial to cats and pot-pie!" he thought to himself. His host spied him, as he crossed the hall, and came out to meet and conduct him into the library, where they were sitting.

"I must introduce you to my niece Robina, the good genius who makes home delightful to me. Robin, my dear, this is my old friend's son."

Conrad prepared to make his best bow to the useful old maid; and then stood so suddenly arrested by surprise that he almost forgot to bow at all.

A tall, graceful girl of some nineteen years stood just within the library door, as they entered, still holding carelessly in one hand the book from which she had been reading. The other hand she reached out instantly and frankly to Conrad. As he took it, he took with it the conviction which most men obtain with greater or less reason at some point in their lives, that this girl was unlike all other girls whom he had ever met.

She greeted him with a real, warm-hearted, old-fashioned smile, — a smile that lingered and brightened in the deep, earnest eyes, and was in itself a satisfactory welcome. At the same time there was a reserve look which said, almost as plainly as words, that her gladness was, as yet, merely a part and because of her uncle's gladness. Whether she would ever give him such a smile solely on his own account would clearly depend upon the ripe estimate which she should form of him, and therefore remained to be proved. In the instant of time during which this stamped itself upon his consciousness as a fact, he also became aware of a strong desire to prove it.

They found out a good deal about one another in the half hour before tea. The parson found out, or imagined he did, that the son of his old friend resembled his father in more than looks. Conrad discovered that young, dark-haired Miss Robin was a vast improvement upon the old, gray-haired Miss Robina he had been led to expect, and boxed Terry's ears mentally for so misleading him ; while the young lady herself, demurely seated in a corner with her sewing, decided that a certain uneasy fear she had cherished in regard to the possible interference with their pleasant home routine of the presence of a " stranger within their gates " was likely to prove unfounded. She slipped from the room presently, leaving the gentlemen to entertain each other for a little, till the small, clear tinkle of a bell struck into their conversation, and put an end to it.

They found the table set for tea on the wide west stoop, and Robin already in her place at its head. It was a trifle strange, perhaps, that the sight of her so placed should carry Conrad back, with a sudden heart-throb, to the time when he could remember his mother, but little older than this girl, who was so young, as she used to smile at him over the big coffee-pot; he perched in his high-chair, miles away it seemed, beside his father.

That was a pleasant meal. The smooth green turf crept to their very feet, and the sunset light flooded all things with a lingering glory; crowning the parson's white head with a rosy nimbus, and bringing out the golden gleams in Robin's wealth of nut-brown curls, as she sat in her big chair and poured tea and cream from the quaint, old-fashioned service into shallow Indian cups, her pretty hands flitting about amongst them like a pair of white butterflies over a bed of blue blossoms.

They lingered long until, when even the parson declared himself unequal to a fourth cup, the table was pushed back through the long window into its place, a servant removed all traces of the repast, and the three new friends sat talking together, while the moonlight brightened and the shadows deepened, far into the evening. Even Robin, under the sweet influences of the night, waxed fearless and talkative, and all unconsciously made herself so irresistible that Conrad found himself watching and listening eagerly for the soft flash of her eyes in the moonlight and the ringing music of her laugh, as the parson told story after story of his college days, and of pranks played by those who were boys then, — dead many of them, or grown old and scarred in fifty years of life's fierce warfare, since.

The laugh died away, and she sat in a subdued silence as he told of his first parish in a large, busy city, and of his young wife and their bright, happy home life and church work together; of how his wife had died and left him with one child, a boy ten years old; and then of how he had come back to the old family farm among the hills, meaning to rear his son to healthy, helpful manhood amid the sweet, strong influences of Nature's solitudes, as the prophets of old and even the Lord himself were reared. "But God had other plans for the boy," said his faithful old minister; "and while I was fitting him for college He was fitting him for heaven. So here I have been, waiting and working ever since. Terry grew up between his grandfather's home and mine, and did me credit at old Harvard. He's a dear boy, a dear boy; but Robin, here, is the staff of my old age!"

and he laid his hand fondly over the dark curls like a crown of praise.

Then the little black clock on the mantel within hammered out ten strokes upon its hidden bell, and they were all surprised to find how late it was. The parson said he was sure Mr. Faulkner must be tired, and Robin brought a lighted candle in a cosy candle-stick ; but smiled as she gave it, saying that he would not keep it burning long. Then he bade them both good-night, and went upstairs, where, sure enough, his first move was to extinguish the candle-flame; for his chamber was flooded through and through with the fair summer moonlight. Away off to the northward rose sharp mountain peaks, with dark, unfathomable shadows lying between. The great elms before the house rustled their green leaves softly against each other, and the sweet breath of the honeysuckle came floating up to him from the porch below.

He rested his arms upon the wide window-sill and gazed far out over the silent panorama spread before him. One by one the lights in the house went out, until there was only one shining from the little vine-hung window in the gable. Suddenly this, too, was extinguished, and the moon and stars had things all to themselves.

Conrad drew in his head with a deep sigh of satisfaction.

"I believe Terry was right," he said to himself; "I believe I am on the right tack now."

CHAPTER III.

CONRAD woke early next morning. He had neglected to close his east blinds before going to bed, and by five o'clock the sun had reached a point whence it could send a well directed shaft into his face, as he lay fronting the window. Even then, had he not opened his eyes, there might have been another chance for him; but he did open them, and after that there was no closing them again.

He rose, therefore, and began a leisurely toilet; enjoying it all immensely from the first splash of the cool, woodsy-smelling water in the big shallow bowl to the final throwing wide of windows and door preparatory to leaving the room.

It was very still. No one seemed to be

astir as yet, but a soft wind moved to meet him as he descended the broad old stairs; and on reaching the hall below he found the door already open, and the fresh breath of the morning pouring in. Early as it was, the bees were up and at work; buzzing in and out among the blossoms, and doubtless making a delicious breakfast upon honey and dew-drops.

He took his hat from the hall table and stepped out upon the gravel. Once there, a little side-path tempted him and he set off to explore its windings. The breeze blew freshly from far-away mountain summits; the long level sun-rays struck to right and left like fairy wands, turning drops of water into flashing jewels; sweet, liquid bird-notes sounded from far and near, and the pines sent forth their spicy summons, not to be denied. The path came to a sudden end. Conrad looked at the tall grass, heavy with moisture, and then at his shining, thin-soled boots. Finally, with a comical grimace, he bent down and rolled the edges of his light summer trousers well out of harm's way; and, plunging boldly into the grassy depths, waded off with great strides toward the woods.

By the time he reached them the sun was well up, and piercing with its myriad golden needles the thick-growing boughs. The trees whispered and laid their heads together above him, and at his feet the brook went flowing by. He remembered how, as a boy at home, he had been wont to follow up the little stream that fed the mill-wheel to its source among the rocks, and how many times he had come back with wet feet, to prim Aunt Hetty's wrath and dismay.

Now his feet were wet already, and Aunt Hetty had been slumbering for many a long year beneath the buttercups and daisies in Winford church-yard. The dry tips of rock poked themselves invitingly above the current, and he accepted their invitation, nothing loth.

Further and further into the woods. No sunshine here, no bird-songs, — nothing but the murmur of the wind among the pines and the ceaseless song of the dancing water.

He climbed on and up, over wet stones and dripping moss, much to the detriment of the aforesaid trousers, till he reached a spot that held him by its wild loveliness and forbade his going further, — a deep, dark rent between the rocks, through which rushed, foaming, the little mountain torrent, leaping with gay abandonment from ledge to ledge, — here dashing headlong, with musical roar, like a mimic cataract; there stealing softly and smoothly over its pebbly bed, or dripping and trickling from the dark, moss - covered walls, — but always hurrying down, down, in its eagerness to reach the rapid river and the great waiting sea.

Just before him, shut in by big boulders, with one fall plunging into it and another rushing from it, lay a pool, — a great round basin, worn by the resistless sweep and swirl of spring freshets into curves and grooves innumerable. Clear beryl-green the water shone in its massive reservoir; and through its cool depths, beneath the shelter of over-hanging rocks, small minnows scurried nimbly to and fro; while an occasional brook trout showed his speckles for a moment, as he glided gracefully past to bury himself in some dark hollow out of reach.

Sight and sound made Conrad thirsty. He stooped and drank of the pure, cold water that had come from miles away, through the darkness of the night.

Something came floating down the brook as he raised his head again. A bit of wood, apparently; not a twig, nor piece of bark such as any brook might gather on its travels; this had shape, — it was larger at one end than at the other, and gleamed white where the bright light touched it, as it came shooting down the fall into the pool. It drifted to one side and lay rocking quietly to and fro, revealing itself as a large wooden spoon. Conrad fished it out. It was graceful in outline, and the handle was rudely carved in a cluster of leaves and fruit.

"How, in the name of all that's sudden, came you here?" he inquired, turning it over in amazement; but the spoon vouchsafed him no reply.

"Seems to me you're a wonderfully shapely chap. Do the farmers' wives hereabouts stir their doughnuts with carved spoons, I wonder?"

His wonder was cut short. Another white gleam shot over the fall, and another spoon lay rocking on the surface of the pool.

"Two spoons! Sign of a wedding, Aunt Hetty used to say. This grows exciting. Hulloa — here comes something else! Some pedler must have come to grief above there."

A shallow wooden bowl came down with a splash and "sailed the ocean blue." After it, echoing gayly from rock to rock, came a sweet ringing laugh. Conrad turned, a spoon in either hand, and beheld Robin standing on a big stone some two hundred feet higher up the brook. She was adorned with a long white linen apron that fell from throat to feet; her sleeves were rolled back, disclosing fair, rounded arms; her pretty hair was carefully tucked away under a little linen cap; and her eyes, looking larger and darker than ever from out so much whiteness, were fairly dancing with merry mischief.

" Good - morning, Miss Cary ! " he exclaimed, transferring a spoon from his right hand to his left and raising his hat, while Robin nodded and smiled in return. "There seems to be quite a brisk trade along shore this morning! Is your stream always as well covered with small craft as now?"

"Not always," replied the girl, while the clear laugh bubbled up again; "this is a boom! 'Three wise men of Gotham went to sea in a bowl.'"

" Ah! where is the third, I wonder? only two dippers - in to science have reached this port. Two — and the bowl!" and Conrad rescued the unlucky vessel as he had its crew, and made his way over the wet stones to Robin's side.

"Thank you very much," said she. holding out her hands to receive the dripping mariners. "The captain, I grieve to say, has probably gone to the bottom. He was my pet skimmer."

"Indeed? poor fellow! he must have been a man of metal, then."

"That he was; and a very hole-y one as well; otherwise he might perhaps have floated, for he was exceedingly broad and thin."

"Broad and thin! an uncommon combination for a sea captain. It will never do to leave such a paradox to his fate. I must fish for him; he can't have got far. Did the — the launch take place here?"

"Just above here, in that little cove. I put them there to soak, but they got away."

"So I perceive. Well, the captain shall not be left to his fate without an effort at a rescue. I will take this branch for a drag, and go to work."

"I must go to work too," said Robin, growing a shade rosier as she remembered for the first time her rather unusual costume. "Don't fish too long. Mr. Faulkner,

— I have other skimmers. If you are successful you will find me at the dairy. It is just in here a little way, at the edge of the woods." And she disappeared, like a white vision, among the trees.

From pool to pool went Conrad, making diligent but unavailing use of his beech-bough drag; and seeing ever before his eyes not a tin skimmer, but a lovely girlish face, with two eyes shining out like stars from under a white cloud of cap-frill.

"I have read of dairymaids, and seen them too," he muttered to himself as he poked and splashed his way down stream, "but I'm blessed if I ever read about" (poke) "or saw" (poke) "a dairymaid like that! It strikes me" — he had reached the big basin again, and was absently stirring its contents round and round like a witch's cauldron — "it strikes me that Miss Robina Cary is a bit unique. Last night in a long dress, with all that rich old lace about her neck and arms, and what novelists call 'a coronet of curls' on her head, she looked like a court lady. This morning in a lank white tyer, — or what would be one on anybody else, — with bare arms and not a curl to be seen, she looks as rosy and demure as one of Wordsworth's little country girls. Which is the reality, I wonder? or is either?"

As there was no one by who could solve this conundrum for him, and as he could not solve it for himself, it presently occurred to him that he might as well hunt up the Enigma and see what she was about. So after one final futile effort to recover what he was in search of, he flung the beech bough away in disgust, and set forth in the direction which Robin had taken.

The dairy at Highfield Farm was a pleasant place into which to find one's way at any time; but at six o'clock of a June morning, when the early breezes came blowing cool over hill - side and pasture, sweet with the breath of wild blossoms and musical with the twittering of hidden birds, to stand before the wide north window, looking down over the green slope to the river, and across the river to other green slopes beyond, was like a bit from some pleasant poem, or like the recalling of a sweet old memory.

Robin was standing thus when Conrad arrived on the spot, having caught through the trees a glimpse of the gilt cow, that formed the vane perched on the tip of the comical red roof, and which, glittering brightly in the early morning sunshine, had served as a guiding star to the young man's willing feet.

She was skimming cream. A six-quart tin stood on the table before her; and, as she swiftly chased and caught the rich yellow cream that fled in heavy, wrinkling folds before her shining skimmer, she transferred it deftly to a great brown-stone crock beside her. She worked on and Conrad watched her. When the first pailful was skimmed she set it off at one side and brought forward another, which also was speedily and skillfully bereft of its rich rising and exchanged for a third.

Evidently she was no novice at dairy-work. There was in every turn and motion of the pretty hands ·that easy dexterity, quick without hurry, which invariably marks the adept at any art. She made so graceful and pleasant a picture that Conrad delayed from moment to moment making his presence known, lest some tinge of consciousness or embarrassment should rob the scene of half its beauty. By and by, however, he became aware that his proximity was no

longer a secret.   A little amused smile began to pucker the corners of the girl's
mouth, and presently she spoke, without
raising her eyes from her work.

" What success, Mr. Faulkner ? "

" Miss Cary ! how did you see me, pray ?
I could take my 'Alfred David' that you
never once raised your eyes," said Conrad,
coming up to the window and answering her
question with another.

" I did not see you — I felt you," said
Robin.   And the eyes, with a laugh in them,
were raised to his face for a moment.   " Do
you never recognize people except with your
eyes ? And where is my skimmer ? 'Is — is
he dead' ? "

" ' Drownd-ed ' " — quoted Conrad in his
turn.   " You see his holey-ness could not
save him."

" Because, like a great deal of so-called
holiness, it would not hold water ! There
are a great many skimmers in the world,
Mr. Faulkner."

" Yes — and a good many strainers, also.
Luckily we are not the tinsmith. Why
don't you ask me to come in, Miss Cary ? "

" Come in by all means, if you like." said
Robin, frankly.   " Do you enjoy a dairy ? "

"To tell the truth, I have never been inside one before," replied the young man, swinging himself lightly to a seat on the broad, low sill. "I have peeped in at a dairy window once, but that was across the water, and the cream had all been skimmed long ago. There were only bare marble tables and a mist of cobwebs or something, that prevented one's seeing even those clearly. Poor little dairymaid! hers was a dangerous dasher. She only meant to stir up butter, but she stirred up a revolution at the same time."

"Trianon!" said Robin, softly; and then said no more for a moment, while her eyes roamed over the fields outside with a dreamy, far-away look, and the corners of her mouth trembled again, ever so little, but not with laughter this time.

It was only for a moment. Even as Conrad watched admiringly the sweet varying face that a word could change from gay to grave, and yet that clearly was the exponent of no weak nature, with its wide, intelligent forehead and firm little mouth and chin, it changed back again in a flash.

"Would you like to learn to stamp butter?"—she sent a bright, arch look full into his face, " because I am just ready to stamp some, and you might help, if you liked."

" I do like — that is, I am sure I shall like, immensely. What must I do first ? "

" Finish getting in, I should say, and then — put these on."

" These " were a pair of long linen sleeves which came up nearly to his shoulders and effectually protected his coat-cuffs.

" Anything else ? " he demanded, leaving his perch on the window-sill and presenting himself at the table whence Robin was busily removing all vestiges of her former occupation. She paused, cream - crock in both hands, and regarded him with a little frown of perplexity.

" I suppose you would feel insulted if I should propose an apron ! "

" Insulted ? not a bit of it. An apron by all means. George Herbert glorified brooms, — why should not aprons be held as honorable ? "

" Why, indeed ? you will find one in the table drawer." And she disappeared through a low doorway into what seemed, looking from the light, a region of total darkness.

When she came back she brought with her, in one hand, a goblet filled with creamy milk; in the other, a wooden trough or tray, which she placed on the table. In it was a great ball of hard, yellow butter.

Conrad did not see this manœuvre. He was busy with his apron, which he put on man-fashion, first tying it tightly about his waist, hind-side before, and then, with a determined grasp of the binding at either side, swinging it round to its proper position, at the imminent risk of cutting himself in two.

"There!" said he, smoothing it down with a sigh of satisfaction; "now what is the next thing to do? I am having a splendid time!"

"Drink this, please. It will be an hour yet before we have breakfast, and I am sure you must be hungry."

"Here's richness!" exclaimed Conrad, as he thanked her and took the goblet. "A city milk-man would feel his digestion ruined forever at the mere sight of such cream."

"Very likely. A prick of conscience often passes for an attack of dyspepsia," laughed Robin, as she produced three wooden prints and three spats which had been soaking in the Gotham bowl, and proceeded to instruct her new pupil in the art of stamping.

" There — first you must draw the handle down so — then pack the butter in with the spat until the mould is full — so. Then smooth it off and do — so!" And with one dexterous punch of the handle she pushed the finished butter - pat out upon the dish placed to receive it.

"How delicious it looks!" said Conrad, bending over the dish in admiration ; " it is a rose, — a golden rose."

"Yes. And you have also a sheaf of wheat, and — what is the other? I forget."

"A butterfly. How suggestive! But what are you going to do yourself? you have given me all the pretty work."

"Not a bit of it! On the contrary I have kept the best for myself." And producing a silver butter-dish she proceeded to cover it with the most delicate golden shells and quirls and hollow scrolls imaginable ; all of which were evolved from solid lumps of butter by some swift, magical manipulation of a pair of wooden spats only differing from ordinary spats in that they were grooved, like a piece of old-fashioned hard gingerbread. When the butter - dish was filled she brought forth from her unfailing cupboards a large platter, which she set herself to covering closely with the same airy constructions. Conrad, getting through with his more solid work first, stood and looked on appreciatively.

"That is high art," he said at length, when the last crumb had been transformed and placed on the dish, — " the beatification of butter. How long will that amount last? there looks to be a week's supply of it."

" Oh, no! that will all be gone by to-morrow night. There is very little to them. They melt away like the most evanescent thing you can imagine."

" Good resolutions," said Conrad.

" Moral butter!" laughed Robin. " A good synonym, Mr. Faulkner. It is time for us to be going now, but, if you like, I will show you over my domicile first."

" Is there more to it then?" said Conrad, glancing round the little octagonal apartment so scrupulously clean and orderly, so sweet and cool with its vine-shaded window and door. " Is n't this the whole?"

" No, indeed, — not half. This is only the shell, the work-room. The kernel of the whole is yet to be exhibited. Where do you suppose all the milk, and cream, and butter are ?"

" There is the butter," he replied. pointing to their finished work. " and when the butter came I suppose the cream departed."

Robin laughed. " Come and see," she said, and disappeared once more through the low doorway into darkness. Conrad paused on the threshold.

" I perceive, Miss Cary, that you take me for a cat. You are mistaken, however. My pupils refuse to expand to the requisite extent."

Robin's low laugh came back to him from out the dusk. " Indeed you are the mistaken one, Mr. Faulkner ! I should object most strongly to encouraging cats in my dairy. Now you can see." And as she spoke a square opening appeared directly ahead, through which the glad light poured in and made things clear.

Stepping down two steps the young man found himself in what appeared to be a small cave, the floor being laid with slabs of gray slate, and the irregular sides formed entirely of huge rocks from whose rough surfaces little streams of moisture were slowly trickling. On a swinging shelf at his right hand were ranged platter after platter like that he had already seen, covered with pats of the same yellow butter. On the floor beneath stood the cream-crock. He looked in vain for anything more.

" You are wondering what has become of the milk," said Robin, — " see here ! " She stooped and lifted a large round grating which was set in the floor, and which, being of the general coloring, had escaped his notice. Beneath was what looked to be a well.

" This is a living spring. Feel how cold the water is." It was cold, almost as cold as ice-water.

" You see I hang my pails down into the spring itself. The animal heat is all out of the milk in a very few minutes, and the cream is magnificent. Look at this ! " She unhooked one of the pails and drew it up. The cream on it was already nearly an inch thick.

" That is twelve hours rising," she said, restoring it to its place. " To - morrow morning I shall skim all these on this side. Those two pails there are for table use. I consider twelve hours long enough for cream that is to be eaten as such to rise. After that it seems to lose something of its fresh taste and become buttery." She put the grating back again, and rose to her feet.

"There are twenty pounds of butter there," she said, glancing with pardonable pride at the golden treasure on the shelf. "To-morrow Abijah will take it over to the Falls, and start it off for Boston, by the early train. Now I will set away the pats which you have been making, and then we must take off our regimentals and go. It is after seven already, and I want to stop for a few lilies of the valley on the way."

"How happens it that you have lilies of the valley in bloom now?" asked Conrad, when the key had been turned on this rustic Paradise and dropped into Robin's pocket, and they were walking away, she with a cream-jug in either hand, and he with the butter-dish. "Is the season so much later here? Miss Constance and I searched in vain, only last week, for enough to make a buttonhole bouquet."

"Management, Mr. Faulkner — management! Women are 'born managers.' you know. I always contrive to keep a patch back for late blooming. They grow in a cool, shady corner by the West Spring."

"Small blame to them! it sounds uncommonly refreshing. Are n't there a good many springs and brooks and things in this favored neighborhood, by the way?"

"Their name is legion," replied Robin, gayly. "There are six brooks and three springs on this farm alone. You see they all cut across our land to get to the river. This large brook is a branch of the river, in fact. It runs into it again about three quarters of a mile below here, so that piece of woodland is really an island. There is a charming view from one end of it, and I have a perch of my own there in a big tree. You might make a sketch from it some day."

"One might spend a lifetime in sketching here in landscape alone, to say nothing of live-stock! Do all the turkeys that I see over there belong to Mr. Cary?" asked Conrad, pointing to myriad black heads that were bobbing about like a school of porpoises in a sea of green grass.

"No, they are mine. And all the chickens that you see over there are mine too. There are my cows just disappearing below the hill. Four of them, — all black. I have a fancy for black cows. I wonder if Marie Antoinette's cows were black, too."

"I never happened to see a black cow in France. The Normandy cattle are mostly red or red and white, and the others that I came in contact with were all mouse-color or creamy-brown, — Jerseys, you know."

" Yes, to be sure : I might have guessed that. How pretty she must have looked in her simple dress, among the mouse-colored cows! One would like to have seen her then. One might have been a great lady, and her intimate friend, you know. But perhaps " —

" Perhaps it is better to live among black cows in New Hampshire? I fancy it is as well. The Queen of France paid for her mouse-color with scarlet; and lilies of the valley are safer, on the whole, than fleurs-de-lis. So — this is the West Spring, I suppose."

The fragrant white bells grew thickly beneath their sheltering leaves, and the pickers' hands were soon filled.

" Now, then," said Conrad, sniffing admiringly at the sweet result of their ten minutes' work, " shall I take one bunch of lilies and two cream-jugs, or one butter-dish and two bunches of lilies, or what ? "

But Robin was too quick for him. She

had hooked one cream-jug on to her little finger, taken the butter-dish in her other hand, and was already on her way again. Nothing remained for him but to take the one bunch and jug that were left and follow.

They hurried up over the green slope together, talking and laughing like two children. Somehow, in the short time that had elapsed since their first meeting, they seemed to have become marvelously well acquainted.

"A wonderfully pleasant phase," thought Conrad, "even if it proves to be only a phase. Last night was pleasant too, though. I wonder which will last?"

It was high time for breakfast when they reached the house, and the parson stood in the porch waiting for them, while near by, armed with a big bell, stood no less a personage than Conrad's stout friend of the stage-coach, clad in crisp calico and evidently very much at home.

"Good morning, Mr. Faulkner! So Robin has pressed you into the service already, hey? She is always an early bird, but you must n't let her impose upon you as she does upon her old uncle." And he tapped the girl's rosy cheek as she ran past him, and beamed after her as if he found being imposed upon rather a pleasant sensation.

"It is an understood thing that the early bird shall always catch the worm, I believe," said Conrad lightly; "it is her perquisite. But the worm has had the best of it this time. He has been learning to make the butter-fly!"

"Good, good! By the way, let me introduce you to our good friend Mrs. Bloom," began his host; but Conrad's hand was already imprisoned, for the second time, in the freckled grasp of that worthy woman.

"You an me's met afore; hain't we, Mr. Forkner? The fust meet was a mighty lucky one fer me, an' I'll try an' see to 't that this ain't an onlucky one fer you. I'm the housekeeper."

"Thank you, Mrs. Bloom," returned Conrad, laughing as he remembered the pot-pie and the cat; "it's a grand thing to be on good terms with the housekeeper, as I know of old. It shall not be my fault, I assure you, if I fall from grace."

"I b'lieve ye!" acquiesced Mrs. Bloom, heartily; adding to the parson, as Conrad passed in, and up to his room, "That's a good young man, ef he is han'sum."

"I believe so," assented the parson, quietly, though his eyes twinkled.

"An' I know so. I ain't be'n married three times fer nothin'. I can read the spellin' in a man's face pretty quick now, I tell ye! an' he's a clean sentence, straight threw. There ain't no bad words in him, nor yet he ain't all question marks an' exclimation p'ints like that feller Terry, neither." And giving the big bell a final brandish, by way of emphasis, Mrs. Bloom hurried in to see that all was as it should be.

Conrad flattered himself that he had been most expeditious when he came down again in irreproachable breakfast-table order. But some one else had been even quicker. There sat Robin in her high-backed chair, making the tea, as daintily attired, as cool, fresh, and quietly composed as if she were now below stairs for the first time that morning, and dairy-work and sunrise rambles were things unheard of.

Indeed, before the meal was over, Conrad was more than ever confirmed in his idea that their previous encounter had been merely a phase, so utterly unlike his rosy

little country girl of an hour ago was this
dignified young woman, presiding at the
head of her uncle's table with all the ease,
and more than all the grace, of a woman
twenty years her senior.

Two people, or sets of people, meet at a
given point in life much as two trains meet
at a station. That they may run together
for a time, however brief, there must be an
interval of switching. And in life, as in
railroad management, so much, either for
safety or danger, depends upon the working
of the switches! Later in the summer Conrad came to realize what a turning-point
that first day at Ockley had been for him.
At the time it was, to all outward seeming,
much like other first days in new places.
They drove, walked, talked, and became acquainted rapidly. For the parson himself
Conrad's respect and liking grew steadily.
He was "right there," as country people
say; genial, sensible and well-read, a devoted mouser among all the old writers and
thinkers, yet ready always with a liberal,
albeit shrewd estimate of the writers and
thinkers of to-day; never ponderous, yet
often weighty; never degenerating either
into sarcasm or silliness, yet blessed with a

keen sense of humor, and finding his quiet amusement in much that, to a more self-ish or conceited person, would have proved merely provoking. A simple, happy-hearted man whose nature was as an open book for all to read who chose. And yet, if any one should fancy he had sounded it to its depths in one such reading, he would find himself most egregiously mistaken.

Conrad, recognizing both these truths, found his liking and veneration for his host momently increasing. As for Robin, he hardly knew what to think. He liked her; oh, yes, he liked her immensely; but she puzzled him. Just such a combination of qualities he had never met with before. Laughing, frolicsome, fairly over-brimming with fun at one moment, grave, quiet, and thoughtful at the next. Ready to enter with intelligent enjoyment into all her uncle's more sober interests and pursuits, or to drop all these, and play with the six variegated kittens that sprawled about in the sunshine after the old tortoise-shell cat. Now giving utterance to some well-formed, pithy opinion, that told of real study and keen insight, anon breaking in upon some discussion that threatened to become too prolonged, with a bit of irresistible drollery that disposed of the question in a flash and sent a laugh stirring, like a fresh summer breeze, among the dry bones of debate. So womanly, when most a child ; so child-like, when most a woman; quaint and queenly at the same time. No wonder that for this first day, and many following, Conrad found himself intent, absorbed, watching and waiting for what the next development should be. The worst of it was that he found himself obliged to relinquish the " phase " theory. It would n't work. One manifestation was as truly Robin as the other, and to save him he could not have told in which mood he liked her best. Character-study was his vocation, and here, he thought, was a character well worth the studying. Accordingly he set himself to the task with praiseworthy devotion.

CHAPTER IV.

Lucy Larcom.

WHAT is there about a country Sunday that is so unmistakable? The sun poured in at Conrad's east window that first Sunday morning just as it had done every other morning since his coming; but it seemed brighter, somehow, and the sky seemed bluer, and the grass greener, than on ordinary days; while the rooster's crowing sounded fainter and more subdued from the barn - yard, and the four black tails of Robin's four black cows apparently found less to excite their lashing activity than usual, as their owners filed slowly down the narrow green lane to pasture. Perhaps the flies were all at Sunday-school.

Over the tops of intervening trees, borne clearly to his ears by the gentle, southerly breeze that always haunted these airy hill-tops, came the sound of church bells. Conrad laid down the pen with which he was filling a sheet to Terry, and leaned back in his chair to listen.

In the great cities, where heavy pavements have crushed all the green, glad life out of poor old Mother Earth, and where high brick walls, and smoke from factory chimneys, have done their utmost to blot from sight the very blue of heaven itself, man's invention, ever restlessly striving to make art supply the place of nature, has given us the chimes, — has broken up swift, white sound into tonic rainbows, that flash and quiver forth from lofty steeples, to break in glad, rhythmic waves over the roofs of homes innumerable, shattering to silence among cold, hard walls, but waking in human hearts, within the walls, echoes sweeter than themselves, of joy and peace.

Up here in the country, chimes were unheard of. Not every meeting - house was sufficiently fortunate to boast even a bell. That in the Ockley steeple was poor enough, little better in quality than such as hang in the belfry of every academy and public school round about our good city of Boston.

Yet, as Conrad sat there listening, the whole world seemed filled with melody. The brave old bell sent forth a peal to the hill-sides, and the hill-sides flung it back to the woods. Peal after peal, and echo after echo meeting, and blending in the warm June air; while ever, as they fainted and died, sweet bird-voices took up the refrain, chanting their glad Te Deum, and the soft wind played among the pines a ceaseless organ accompaniment. With so many distractions Conrad's letter progressed but slowly. As he completed and placed it in its envelope a new sound blended with the general harmony outside, — the sound of wheels on gravel. The tall, antique chaise in which the parson was wont to take placid jogs about the neighboring country stood before the door; and by peeping between the honey-suckle sprays, Conrad could see Robin and her uncle preparing to mount. The former paused, with one foot on the step, and turned her head for a parting word with Mrs. Bloom, who stood in the door-way.

"Tell Mr. Faulkner, please, that Abijah will drive back for him in time for church."

The young man referred to thrust his head out among the clustering vines, and called down : —

"Abijah need not do that, Miss Cary! I have so much time that I think I will stroll along at my leisure presently. Old Nahum will doubtless agree with me as to its being the better plan."

"Do you really prefer it?" asked the parson, looking up in his turn. "The horse can come back as well as not."

"I really prefer it, thank you. It is just the day for a walk. Miss Cary, will you walk back with me?"

"With pleasure, Mr. Faulkner. There is a bumble-bee on your head!" and the bright face in the pretty bonnet extinguished itself beneath the lumbering chaise-top.

Conrad's head maintained its position, despite the bumble-bee, for several minutes longer. Its owner almost began to think that the bee must be in his bonnet, instead of merely lumbering about with unsteady, pollen-laden legs over the thick, wavy crop of his brown-hair. Else why was it that he so often nowadays found himself mooning away his time as he was doing at this identical juncture, his eyes riveted to the cracked leather of the old chaise-top, and all his wits gone wool-gathering? He had never done so before. Surely there must be something in Ockley air that exercised an unusually soothing influence upon the nerves.

Whatever that something might be it ceased to act, apparently, as soon as the chaise and old Nahum were lost to sight in the hollow below the hill. The head was drawn back quickly, dislodging the bee, who gave vent to his feelings of wounded dignity in an angry hum, and the owner of it, whistling softly to himself the while, proceeded to make ready for church.

The bell was again ringing from the square white tower when Conrad reached the village, an hour later. The church itself was empty ; it would be fifteen minutes before service began, and he amused himself by strolling up one aisle and down another, glancing at the names on the hymn-books, and enjoying the cool breeze that stole in through green, closed blinds. On the stained-wood table before the pulpit was a great bunch of Robin's lilies. He had seen them in her hand, when she turned to look up at him, as he stood at his window.

All at once there came a sound of singing from the basement below. Sunday-school was over, and the people would be flocking in directly. He made his way to the pew in which the hymn-books bore the name "Cary" stamped in gilt letters upon their faded binding, and which, he was relieved to find, did not follow the custom prevalent in most country churches of being directly under the pulpit, but was a little back, where one might see the preacher's face occasionally without incurring cramp in the back of the neck, or rolling one's eye-balls up into indefinite regions at the risk of never bringing them down again in safety. Sitting here while the farmers and the farmers' wives, their sons and their daughters, poured in in a steady stream till the little church presented the appearance of a gay, old-fashioned flower-garden, the bright bonnets and shawls of the women, contrasted and set off by the sunbrowned faces of their husbands and brothers, as hollyhocks look all the more glowing and brilliant for growing against an old picket-fence, he was suddenly aware of a low, stealing melody that seemed borne in on the June air with the scent of roses from the green graveyard outside. He knew it, it was a bit from Schumann.

There could surely be but one person here who would play such music as that. He was not surprised, when he turned and looked up at the gallery, to see Robin's delicate summer dress peeping out between the broad shoulders and showy ribbons in the " singers' seats." It did surprise him somewhat to behold Cy, in decorous Sabbath attire and with hair sleeked smooth to his head, arduously pumping away at the organ bellows, his eyes, as well as his exertions would permit, fastened on Robin's face, and so lost in the music as to be often near forgetting the important part he was himself playing in its production. Conrad's pleasure in the organist's skill was sadly marred by his constant uneasiness lest Cy should stop blowing altogether.

The parson preached a quiet, forcible sermon, the singers rendered the three hymns with an enthusiasm which should have gone far to atone for any lack of harmony, the benediction was at last pronounced, and the flower-garden emptied itself from the shady shelter of the church into the warmth and sunshine without. Robin, coming down last of all with Cy, met Conrad at the foot of the gallery stairs.

" Cy," she said, laying one gloved hand on the fat boy's arm to draw attention to her words, " this is my — this is Mr. Faulkner."

Cy grunted.

"Cy and I have met before," said Conrad, doing his best to suppress a smile, and holding out his hand more for the sake of not seeming to slight Robin's introduction than because he felt any attraction to the boy himself. A moment later he was glad he had done so, for Cy's look, as he hesitatingly laid his own within it, and instantly withdrew it again, smote him half reproachfully with its wistful questioning. The poor fellow could not be so utterly unlike other people after all, since he had wit enough to feel the difference so keenly.

"I am glad you did that," said Robin, gathering her light draperies about her from the dusty way as they walked off up the road together, leaving Cy sitting on the low graveyard wall, whence he followed them with his eyes till they were out of sight. "Cy has quick feelings either for a kindness or the reverse, and although there are always plenty of people ready to amuse themselves with him, and many more to patronize or pity, there are very few who would meet him on equal ground as kindly and cordially as you did."

Her words pricked Conrad's conscience

even more sharply than Cy's look had done ;
but then, on the other hand, they made him
gladder too.

"They call Cy a fool," went on the girl,
gravely, with a quick, earnest look into his
face as if demanding of him a truer judgment, "but that is a mistake. He was a
mere child when he met with a terrible accident, and — he has stayed a child, that is
all."

"I see," said Conrad, quietly ; and they
walked on for some moments in silence.

From time to time the young man stole a
look at his companion, unobserved. There
seemed to be a peculiar charm about her to-
day, somehow. Was the same intangible
Sunday influence which he had already felt
in other things at work here also, making
the sweet face more winning than ever in
its grave beauty ? Or was it — could it be ?
— the bonnet ! He had never seen her in a
bonnet before.

Somehow, in this particular instance, character-study was proving a failure. All his
observations of late seemed to be taking the
direction rather of recognition and approval
than of detection and analysis. From having begun by thinking what a fresh, piquant

heroine she would make for a book, of which he should be the inspired author, he had unconsciously come to feel as if they were both in a book together, and the author were making them, or him at any rate, think and feel and act about as he pleased.

Ah, he is a mighty author, and an acute! that little fellow, with a quiver for an inkstand, who points his sentences with sharp and noiseless arrows. The book is always of the "No Name Series," too: Mr. Cupid is a skillful novelist. We are allowed to read far on in our pleasant little romance before any inkling of the plot's irresistible drift dawns upon us. Then, of a sudden, some memorable day it comes! that breathless moment of divination when we know, beyond all possibility of doubt, that but one of two endings can be. Will it be joy? Will it be destruction? Read, and see. There is no such thing as pausing, no such thing as skipping; the pages slip a little faster, that is all. One more leaf to turn and the whole drift of life is turning with it. Our good friends, who are always ready to do their little bit of over-shoulder reading, whether it be tragedy or love-tale, exchange sagacious nods, and go their way to guess and prophesy as to the final winding up. All but one, the one. Only two pairs of eyes may read the rest, only two hearts shall ever know what were the words of blessedness or pain with which the fateful volume closed.

Stories that end well, stories that end ill, stories that never end at all; the bookshelves of the world are full of them. Happy the heart that, looking with love-strengthened eyes beyond the gloom of earth's black " Finis," can read, a little further on, heaven's bright "To be continued! "

Conrad was still in the early half of his book. That it was the work of no novice he felt, rather than understood, but as yet he did not recognize the hand. The interest was growing, decidedly; this, for instance, was an exceedingly pleasant page.

He smiled a little, half unconsciously, over his own fanciful conceit, and Robin caught him at it.

" It would be too hackneyed to make the usual offer of 'a penny,' Mr. Faulkner; suppose I were to offer this, instead," and she laughingly held out a wild strawberry which she had that moment spied among the grass.

“Thoughts are seldom unmixed,” said Conrad, twirling the scarlet fruit upon its slender stalk, “they are mostly ‘human warious.’ I believe I was rather absorbing than thinking. Such weather is enough to make a mental sponge of a man. Do you like wild strawberries, Miss — Robin ? ”

“You do not, apparently,” replied she, flushing a little at the new name, and glancing significantly at the berry in his hand.

“Oh, yes, I do; I like them exceedingly ; but why did you not answer my question ? ”

“If I were to say yes, you would probably request me to eat that one.”

“N-no, I hardly think so,” said Conrad, dubiously ; “it is too pretty to eat alone. If there were a saucerful it would be another thing. But what if I did ? ” he added, abruptly, “why should n’t you ? ”

“Because I never take back a thing when I have once given it.”

“Another trait. Do you know, I am finding new traits in your character all the time.”

“Is n’t that rather to be expected when one makes a new acquaintance ? ”

“Ah, thank you ! ” exclaimed he ; “ that reminds me. I knew something was haunting my memory. Now for it! Why did you leave out a word when you introduced me to Cy?"

"What word?" began Robin, in astonishment, and then instantly remembered. He saw by the dropped lids and quick color that she knew what he meant, and waited, with that bending, masterful look into her face by which the question masculine is wont to compel the reply feminine.

If he expected evasion or denial he was disappointed. Robin always took a dilemma by the horns. There was neither fear nor falsity in the clear eyes when she raised them again to his face.

"I began to call you my friend," she said, quietly; "and then I remembered."

"Remembered what? Not that I am your enemy, I hope?"

An amused little smile was her only answer.

"I see," said Conrad, "you attach some very deep meaning to that word ' friend.' "

"Don't you?"

He shook his head; not exactly in denial, either.

"I am sadly afraid that I have always used the word with rash indiscrimination. You must teach me better."

"Now you are laughing, and I am in earnest." There was a little ring of disappointment in her voice. Conrad's face changed instantly.

"Indeed I was not laughing. Or, if I was, it was only a surface laugh. Miss Robin, I never had a friend, a near friend, in my life. Miss Constance and her brother are the only people who care especially about me, and they are more like parents than friends. You must not wonder if I hardly know what the word means. What does it mean?"

Robin was silent from sheer pressure of speech.

"Well, if you won't tell me," said Conrad, lightly, "I must consult Webster;" and he drew from his pocket a little traveling dictionary.

"Fl— Fo— Fr— here it is. Now listen!" and coming to a halt by the roadside, he read the definition.

"'Friend. One who, entertaining for another sentiments of esteem, respect, and affection, from personal predilection seeks his society and welfare.' There, how is that?"

"Good, — as far as it goes."

"Does n't it go far enough?"

" Not for me."

" What more do you require ? "

" The impossibility of a misunderstanding."

" Is such an impossibility possible ? "

" I think so," said Robin slowly, poking a stray pebble with her sun umbrella, and watching the operation intently, " if two people never allow a third to interfere, and if they do all their ' wondering ' aloud. There can be no real friendship without entire confidence."

" That is indisputably so. I accept your amendment. Dr. Webster stands convicted of a grave omission. But after all this it comes rather hard to remember that you will not call yourself my friend."

" You misunderstood me," said Robin quietly. " I only meant .that it was not my place to assume the friendship."

" Or, in other words, ' it takes two to make a bargain,' " said Conrad, gayly; " shall we make one ? "

Then, as Robin still kept silence, he drew a step nearer and held out his hand.

" Miss Robin, as I told you just now, I have never in all my life known what it was to have such a friend as you " — he smiled,

— "and Dr. Webster describe. If you will be my friend I promise you solemnly that I will never misunderstand you again, and that I will on no account whatever believe a single word that any third person may say."

There was a tone in his voice that gave weight to the light, surface words, and Robin's eyes, in the swift scrutiny with which they were raised for a moment to his, detected apparently the underlying earnestness they sought; for, without another word, she drew her right hand from its loosened glove, and laid it frankly and unhesitatingly in his.

Strange, that the mere touch of a girl's hand should have power to send such a glad throb from heart to brain. There was a wonderful shine all at once in the handsome brown face turned toward her. But Robin's eyes were down, and she did not see it, neither could he behold their tender mistiness beneath the veiling lids; and the cool rose of her cheek told no tales. They climbed the last long hill together very slowly and silently.

Worthy Mrs. Bloom, issuing from the porch door with her big bell, saw them coming; and it was with a most shrewd and knowing expression of countenance that she presently went in again, without ringing, and deposited her noisy coadjutor upon its customary bracket by the dining-room door.

" There ! " she exclaimed softly, with a warning nod to her own reflection from its shiny brass surface. " You hold your tongue, an' I 'll hold mine."

So it happened that when the two reached the porch they found it untenanted, save by the restless breeze that stirred the honey-suckle blooms to fragrance.

" Remember, Miss Robin," said Conrad, as they parted at the stair head ; " I have your own word for it that when you have once given a thing, you never take it back."

7

CHAPTER V.

Lowell.

THE bright hours rolled themselves together like drops of quicksilver. They gathered to days, and the days to weeks. Life was at compound interest in the bank of enjoyment, — that queer bank where capital doubles and trebles with such amazing velocity that one comes to be a millionaire in happiness before one is well aware. Alas for the man who thinks to cash his check in this strange currency at will! Old Father Time is an absconding cashier, and at the flood tide of prosperity the too trustful depositor finds the doors closed against him. The bank has suspended payment!

Conrad Faulkner was not a pauper yet, by any means. On the contrary, he was in that first, delicious flush of fortune when both hands fairly overflow with golden opportunities for self-selected work and play.

He was writing his first novel, and who-
ever has tried it knows that to be suddenly
let loose from the treadmill of literary job-
work to roam, unimpeded, over the limitless
pastures of one's own imagination, is a sensation unparalleled and indescribable. His
pastures were uncommonly fresh and juicy,
too. Robin and the parson, with their keen
appreciation of all things original and quaint,
and their wide experience of country life
and ways, proved able and interesting as-
sistants. Many a long jaunt did the two
gentlemen take in the old chaise together,
and many a queer characteristic, or spicy
bit of dialogue, found its way into Conrad's
note-book, as the result of these morning
drives. And while his note-book fattened
on the bountiful fare provided for it, his
sketch-book kept even pace. Robin herself
dabbled in water-color, and many a valuable
bit was transferred to paper to be worked
up more fully at some leisure moment in the
future.

But if the young man's writing hours
were uninterrupted, and his progress toward
the temple of Fame reasonably swift and
sure, it was often through no merit of his
own. Many a time did the parson laugh-

ingly turn his back upon him, and refuse to talk until working hours were over, while Robin would retreat to the kitchen upon the stroke of nine, and never reappear within his range of vision until dinner was on the table.

Mrs. Bloom had been as good as her word. In her own peculiar province, she put forth all her energies to render herself agreeable to the parson's guest, who found many another savory dish, as well as the celebrated pot-pie, served up for his especial benefit from her inexhaustible repertory of delectable fare.

He had grown intimate with Cy, too (who had never forgotten their meeting in the church porch, and would have gone through fire and water for " Miss Robin's friend "), and had found that the fat boy's friendship was well worth cultivating, for more reasons than one. Cy knew where all the trout-holes were, and where the rarest flowers and ferns were to be found. He could always tell of a short cut to any desired locality ; and, after successfully piloting Conrad to the very most desirable point for a required sketch, was always ready to lie, for hours if need were, upon the grass beside the camp-stool, his eyes roaming from the artist's face to his developing work, thence away, over the landscape it portrayed, and back to Conrad's face again. Thus, reading out of the one grand book together, they came to read each other truly, too. The young man found, behind the stunted outward seeming of him they called a fool, a wealth of fine perception, a treasure of warm-hearted loyalty, that added reverence and amazement to his pity. He found a soul shut in upon itself, and not a soul benumbed; while Cy, on his part, looked up to his patron as to a strong, wise angel who could do no wrong.

Conrad had now been for three weeks at Highfield Farm. At the end of the fortnight which was to have brought July and Terry together to the hills, the former appeared promptly, but in lieu of the latter came a mournful epistle to say that either out of spite, or from too high living, old Crabbe had "gone and got a fit of the gollywobbles, and was laid up at home to the mutual misery of his housekeeper and himself (Terry), who could not leave his grandfather to shoulder things alone." Upon this, feeling himself called upon to act, Conrad heroically announced his intention to depart; but he soon found that he had reckoned literally without his host. The parson was severely deaf to any such proposition.

Was he tired of Ockley? had he exhausted its resources both for literature and art, or was urgent business calling him away?

No, he could plead none of these excuses.

Then why did he want to go?

Upon which the young man spoke out valiantly for the truth, and said, —

" I don't want to go ! "

"Then stay," commanded the parson, visibly pleased with his guest's candor. "And stay as long as business and pleasure will let you. We usually flit to the city ourselves about Thanksgiving time, to give Robin here a taste of worldly pomps and vanities; but so long as we remain you are more than welcome. And if you wanted to paint the hills in mid-winter, Mrs. Bloom would only rejoice to make you comfortable. Moreover, you are under contract to wait for Terry."

So Conrad stayed, and was rewarded by one of Robin's most radiant smiles, all on his own account this time.

Waiting for Terry bid fair to prove an all-summer amusement. Terry could not get away. Business had "picked up," in spite of his prognostications to the contrary, and old Crabbe, not mellowed apparently by his forced sequestration, had fastened his mercenary claws upon him, and held him fast. August would be dull. He might have the whole of August if he wanted it, but not a day in July. So Terry succumbed, to his credit it must be owned, since he need not have remained an hour behind his grandfather's desk had not his sense of duty, and the strong desire to be a man, which lay hidden beneath all his boyishness, held him to his post by bands of might. Doleful notes found their way, from time to time, from the weary world of traffic into the upper peace of Saints' Rest, where, it must be confessed, two at least of the beatified evidenced the extreme narrowness of the line dividing saint and sinner by the ready serenity of their acquiescence in the ordained order of things as regarded their suffering friend below. To be sure, on warm afternoons when Robin brought her work out under the trees, while Conrad sketched or lounged, and the parson read aloud to them both, there would come a momentary twinge of conscience as they thought how insufferable the heat must be in city counting-houses and upon the glaring wharves. But the breeze from the mountains blew soft and refreshing in spite of the thermometer, and the parson gave them such delicious bits from his old, leather-bound English cronies, that even conscience itself was charmed to rest; and the old Adam so far got the upper hand as to rejoice that their happy trio was not yet broken up into a quartette.

Our hero was fast gaining such an insight into the true and possible meaning of the word "friendship" as made him wax well-nigh contemptuous of the abilities of our modern Noah. After all, neither an ark nor a dictionary will hold everything. The Patriarchs did their best; but Robin was not a patriarch, neither was she tied down by any limitations of space. The whole universe of thought and life was hers through which to define the one word that had been given her. And such an unconscious, winning grace pervaded her every fresh manifestation that, half unwittingly to himself, the word began to condense in Conrad's mind, and to spell itself with four letters instead of ten.

He always rose with the sun now. Having had a taste of the early bird's worm, the appetite for more grew to a craving. Many a pound of butter passed through his hands on its way from churn to market. He grew to be as expert with the spats as Robin herself; and the invention and execution of novel and unique designs came to be a matter of rivalry between them. The dairy was transformed into a studio, and the parson declared that the breakfast - table was fast degenerating into a mixture of the Place de la Concorde and the South Sea Islands, so numerous were the illustrious martyrs there decapitated by the butter-knife and devoured on muffins and waffles.

" I am thinking," remarked the reverend gentleman one morning as he thoughtfully cut a generous slice from the back of Savonarola's head and handed it across the table to Conrad, " I am thinking of taking a run down to Deake to-day."

" Give me his nose, please, Uncle Ike, if you are helping me. I would rather eat it than look at it. There 's something wrong about the hook."

" That comes of trying to distinguish your-self, ' by hook or by crook.' For my part, I believe I prefer flowers to folks when it comes to butter. This eating a monk for breakfast, and a queen for dinner, and mak-ing a Herod of one's self at night, savors too strongly of moral dyspepsia. But about this going to Deake. You won't mind my being away for a day, and that trust busi-ness ought to be attended to. I shall go to the clearing first to consult with Miss Doris, and then take the train at the Cross Roads. Abijah can drive me over and bring the horse back, and while he is there he may as well get the cutter-bar mended. We shall need it next week."

" Abijah was going over to the South Pas-ture this forenoon to salt the cattle."

" So he was ! And that should be done right away. Abijah will need to use Nahum this afternoon, too, otherwise I might keep him all day. Well, I can put off my busi-ness to a better time, I suppose."

" No need of that," said Conrad, " why cannot I drive you over as well as Abijah, and get the cutter-bar mended, too ? "

" To be sure ; so you could. The drive is a pleasant one. Only I fear you might get tired of waiting for me. The Misses Cleppitt are rather lengthy in conversation, and I shall have to do just about so much talking."

"And I don't believe an hour's *tête-à-tête* with Nahum would be very exhilarating," added Robin. "Mr. Faulkner, if you take my advice, you will explore the old graveyard there. There are some epitaphs that would make a newspaper man's fortune. Only you must not put any of them into your book; every one does that nowadays."

"Well, really my dear!" exclaimed the parson in mild remonstrance, "if it comes to a question of exhilaration between Nahum and a graveyard, give me the horse, by all means!"

Conrad and Robin laughed, but the latter did not yield her point.

"A burying-ground is composing, at all events, and there is nothing composing about Nahum in fly-time. Besides, Mr. Faulkner, this one that I speak of is really interesting. It is a relic of by-gone times."

"So is Nahum," put in the parson. "However, Conrad, since she says so you may as well yield the point with a good grace. You will have to come to it. It's to be hoped you enjoy burying-grounds."

“I do, rather. I spent an evening last summer in one at the foot of Monadnock, and felt half inclined to take up my abode there for good and all.”

“I should judge it was through no fault of yours that you did not,” remarked the parson, dryly, with a shrug of his broad shoulders. “When your bones get to be as old as mine you won’t throw them round among damp sods quite so recklessly. But come! if you have eaten as much of that gentleman’s back hair as you care to, and won’t take another muffin, let us be going. It’s not a long drive, but Job Curtis will want all the time there is between this and dinner.”

“Uncle Ike! you betray a degree of ignorance which is simply shocking,” said Robin, gazing tenderly at Savonarola’s golden relics. “Monks don’t have any back hair.”

“No, I believe, come to think of it, they make it all up into shirts. Uncomfortable that must be, very. But, my dear child, was that really intended for a monk, or was it — a monkey?” And the parson fled, just in time to escape the rose which Robin threw at him from the basket in the centre of the table.

"Did ever any one see so undignified a Dominie! Really, Mr. Faulkner, there is no such hurry. It always takes Abijah fifteen minutes to harness. Won't you have something more?"

"Nothing but this," stooping, as he spoke, to pick up the rose which lay on the floor. "What do you mean to do with yourself this morning?"

"Make a strawberry short-cake for your dinner, for one thing. This is baking-day."

"Baking it will be in more senses than one, I fancy. Would you not do better to omit the short-cake?"

"You may answer that question when dinner-time comes," said Robin, following him to the porch. "Be sure to find Launcelot Owen's gravestone. I will tell you more about him one of these days. Good-by, Uncle Ike. You shall have Louis Fourteenth for your supper, wig and all!"

"So be it, my dear," responded her uncle submissively. "His wig will be easier to digest than his morals. I shall rather enjoy giving the old fellow a bite. Take good care of yourself, little girl, and try to make the day pass pleasantly for our friend. Get up, Nahum!"

These drives were the most restful and entertaining things, in their way, that Conrad had ever participated in. Nahum was a vastly different specimen of horseflesh from the blooded roans, and bays, and chestnuts driven by various of his New York acquaintances; and yet, under certain circumstances, there is a rare, peculiar pleasure in jogging about the country after a scrubby old nag such as he. A horse, especially a family horse, is generally one of two things by the time he rounds his twentieth year. He is either a wise beast or a dead one. Nahum had chosen the former alternative, as became the namesake of a prophet. He was very wise. In some matters the parson was a mere baby beside him. He had a sharp nose for a parishioner. Wagon after wagon might pass unnoticed if its owner were a stranger; but let one heave in sight containing a member of his, and his master's, legitimate flock, and the knowing beast would draw up alongside and come to a dead halt, well assured that the parson was not to be let by without a prolonged " word or two." There were certain door-yards which he could never be persuaded to pass unvisited, certain others which he could hardly be induced to enter; while invariably, as they drew near the village store where Mrs. Bloom did her " trading," he would turn one questioning eye upon his driver as if to ask, " Have we any errand here to-day ? "

Conrad had already clapped him into his book, and daily studied him, as he would a human being, for fresh developments of character.

The roads radiating from Oakley, as a centre, were well-nigh innumerable. This morning they took one which Conrad had never traveled before, and struck off, north-ward, into the very heart of the hills. Up one side of a steep ridge in the hot sunshine of a day which promised to be a veritable scorcher by noon; down the other side into coolness, and shadow, and a green pervad-ing peace. Now through some small settle-ment, where the only notice bestowed upon trees had been to hew them down, and chop them into firewood, great piles of which sent forth a resinous breath, in dying remon-strance, beneath the remorseless sun; again, into the solemn minster-gloom of dense pine woods where the sunshine durst not pene-trate, and where the only sounds audible were the songs of birds, and the softened thud of Nahum's big hoofs upon a century-piled carpet of brown needles.

"There!" exclaimed the parson, as a horse and buggy approached them through the trees, driven by a spare, solemn-looking man in black clothes, "that is Mr. Neal, the Methodist minister. I wanted to speak with him about a union meeting next week. Whoa, Nahum! whoa, sir!"

But Nahum only shook his wary old head, and jogged stubbornly along. The man in black bowed, very cordially, in passing, and forgot to look solemn for a moment.

"Well — well, perhaps I shall see him at his house on the way back. To tell the truth," explained the parson, looking a trifle sheepish, "Nahum has a most unaccountable prejudice against Methodists. In the whole two years that Mr. Neal has been here I have never yet been able to get a word with him on the road. I sometimes think the brute is getting to be one too many for me. See how he listens! He knows what I am saying as well as you do."

Upon which Nahum, who had been cocking one ear back with an attentive air, immediately restored it to its normal position, and trotted on, the picture of meek sedateness.

It was strange how the villages belied
their names. Through Woodside, and Pleas-
anton, and Fairview, — places destitute alike
of shade and beauty, — they came at length
to Cleppitt's Clearing, a broad, level street,
lined on either side with noble forest trees,
behind which stretched away well-kept farms,
the undulating land hidden from view by its
wealth of grain and close-growing grasses,
save where the busy mowing-machines were
fast shearing away the waving green, and
leaving a smooth, clean carpet in its stead.

"If it were not that the ladies Cleppitt
are never prepared to entertain any one,
even an angel, unawares, I should propose
your going in with me," said the parson.
"The house is well worth seeing. One of
these days Robin must introduce you, having carefully notified the worthy ladies be-
fore-hand. She is prime favorite with the
sisters. Whoa, Nahum! This is where we
leave the cutter-bar. Job," — as a spare,
bent, sinewy old man came slowly from the
shady covert of the vine-hung smithy at
whose door they now drew up, — " I want
you to be sure to have this done within an
hour. You can do it easily, if you choose.
This gentleman will call for it."

The old man took the cutter-bar from the chaise and carefully scrutinized it. Then he bent a sharp, searching gaze upon Conrad from over his iron - bowed spectacles; and, turning, walked back into his smithy without a word.

"Another character!" quoth the parson, starting on again. "The place is full of them."

The houses, standing mostly on one side of the street, with their several tillage and mowing pieces on the other, were evidently old, yet built with a careful solidity which defied age. They were many - gabled too, and well supplied with quaint, unexpected angles. About most of them the rich, velvety turf bore witness to an amount of culture not often bestowed upon grass — as such — by our native farmers; and the faint, delicious scent of box stole from hidden garden-spaces beyond.

"Surely Cleppitt was an Englishman!" was Conrad's only spoken comment, as they jogged slowly along under the green arcade.

"And you are as surely a Yankee! Your guessing faculty is thoroughly well developed," laughed the parson. "But come now, — tell me how you knew."

"By three infallible signs. The typical New Englander can never get among trees without running a regular muck. Grass is of no value in his eyes, except as it stocks his barns with hay. Above all, — he acknowledges no angle save a right-angle."

"Robin's reasoning, to a dot! I declare, it's queer how like you two are in your ways of thinking. You're not far wrong. Cleppitt was a Welshman. He came here some hundred years ago, and set to work to turn a piece of New Hampshire into a piece of Wales. Succeeded pretty well, too. His brothers, and his wife's relatives came over and joined him, and among them they made the place pretty much what you see it is now. You see these Welshmen did n't approve of pine wood for building purposes, so, as soon as they conveniently could, they set to work to build houses that would last. You notice that all these which you see are built of stone. It's the law of the place, laid down by will from father to son. Another stipulation is that the places themselves shall always be kept up in the old way. Well, it has been done, so far; but the new generation that is coming up now has considerable of the Yankee element in it, and we all know that the Yankee element is pretty strong. These particular homesteads will probably hold their own as long as they last; but the town will gradually grow mixed, especially as the youngsters buy up new land for themselves, and I rather guess that if David Cleppitt's ghost tries to walk about much o' nights, he will stumble over some wooden houses before long. Whoa, Nahum!"

The parson always said "Whoa!" It had grown to be a habit with him, much as stopping when he reached his destination had grown to be a habit with the old horse. Sometimes the parson got the start of Nahum, but oftener Nahum got the start of the parson. He had done so now; and, when the tardy word of command reached his ears, was already rubbing his nose against a well-worn hitching-post which stood, like some ancient sentry, before the gateway of the oldest house they had yet seen. He took no notice of his master's idiosyncrasy, however, but merely turned a slow and placid backward look upon Conrad, as who should say, "He's a trifle queer at times, but he means well," and then, stretching his long neck which no check-rein was ever allowed to cramp, fell quietly to munching the tufts of juicy clover at his feet.

"Now I am going in here," said Mr. Cary, "and you, I suppose, are bound for the graveyard. No need to lose your way. You'll find it right ahead, at the end of the road, as we all shall, sooner or later! Old Cleppitt seems to have been of a typical turn of mind, and to have laid out his clearing like a kind of bird's-eye view of human life. Good-by, for a time!" and the parson opened the tall, Gothic gate, and went his way.

There was no trouble about finding the graveyard, certainly. The trouble would have been to avoid it. Square across the broad, pleasant street it stretched itself; the end of all things, literally as well as figuratively, at Cleppitt's Clearing; its wide, stone entrance standing, like the arch of the Star, to commemorate a conqueror's triumph.

Conrad involuntarily removed his hat as he passed beneath the massive portal. There is something about an archway which impels one to this act of reverence. A hen is no such fool when she bobs at the barn-door. It is but the universal instinct stirring within

her and not, as some people would have it,
a mere feminine fear for the safety of her
coral-comb.

Peaceful as the whole of the little settle-
ment seemed, a deeper peace, a more abid-
ing hush had fallen upon the old inhabit-
ants in their restful graves. The very
stones themselves, gray and moss - grown,
leaned and slumbered at their posts. Some,
for which the drowsiness of years had
proved too powerful, lay prone amid the
waving grass - blooms, like Ibrahim Ebn
Abu Ayub in his subterranean cave ; while
the clover blossoms nodded dreamy heads
above them, and the summer wind, like a
fair enchantress, lulled them to forgetful-
ness with her magic music.

Quaint old place, quaint old stones,
quaint old epitaphs ! Ludicrous enough,
many of them. A newspaper man's fortune, as Robin had said. Yet, somehow,
here where they belonged, where the old-
time influences and the spirit of the old-time
originators made a nameless atmosphere
about them, they were not to be laughed at
exactly.

The hour allotted to Job Curtis had
grown to be nearly two hours when the

parson, having concluded his consultation with Miss Doris, came to look up his guest, and found him half-lying in the cool, fragrant grass, back to back with a tombstone. In his hands pencil and paper, and in his eyes the far-away look of one who has *treed* an idea, and is wondering how he shall get it down.

"Come, come! this is not so bad, young man. Inspired already! Old Nahum looked uncommonly solemn as I passed him just now. I had small hope of finding you till I saw him still standing there. It seems Robin knew her ground when she declared a graveyard to be 'a composing sort of place.' But to be first-class your epic needs a hero. Have you found Launcelot Owen, yet?"

"No, I have n't!" exclaimed Conrad, springing to his feet and exchanging the abstracted gaze of genius for the more concentrated one of eager search. "I meant to have had another look presently, but somehow time has fairly flown since I have been down here in the grass."

"Or up there in the clouds, hey? Well, you are but another living instance of the way in which people turn their backs upon the very things they are looking for. Suppose you examine the face of this stone which you seem to have had such a leaning towards."

Conrad walked round to where the parson stood, and then perceived that what he had been leaning against was a plain, moss-grown tablet of slate, simply inscribed as follows : —

LAUNCELOT OWEN.

DIED FEBRUARY 15, 1801,

Aged 40 years.

Beneath were six short lines. Conrad was obliged to stoop and scrape the moss away to read them.

> " God gave me a hard daye's worke;
>   But I did not shirke.
> Toe them that doe theyre beste,
>   He hath promised reste.
> Soe now I 'll creepe toe my bedde,
>   And truste him, livinge or deade."

" Who was he ? " asked Conrad, when he had read the words over for the second time ; " no ordinary man."

" He was the poet of the neighborhood. The only one it ever boasted, I fancy. People came to him, for miles around, to furnish epitaphs, occasional verses, and the like. For the rest he was a farmer ; grand-uncle of the two old ladies whom I have just been calling upon. Robin can give you his whole history. He is a hero of hers. But now I shall have to hurry you away from this congenial atmosphere if we are to catch the train."

Old Nahum turned a deeply reproachful look upon them as they came up to where he stood, the parson having fetched him along, and left him waiting near the cemetery gate.

"We keep on a bit, to the station," said, the latter gentleman, as he gathered up the reins. "There is a small settlement over beyond here, known to the unregenerate as Paradise, because one is obliged to pass through the graveyard to get to it. The locomotives stop there for water."

There was a train just drawing away from the big water-tank as they reached the cross-roads. The parson slid nimbly from the chaise and gained the rear platform.

"Good-day!" he shouted. "Don't wait for Job, if he is not ready. Abijah can stop there later."

The train puffed away, and Conrad, turning his horse's head, drove back to the smithy.

The old smith gave him another look over his spectacles as he came in. The cutter-bar was lying on the floor, untouched. Job was tinkering up an old andiron. If he had expected the gentleman to make any remarks he was disappointed. Conrad satisfied himself that the bar was as it had been, and then, without even a second glance toward the recusant proprietor of the premises, turned on his heel and walked away. A low, toothless chuckle sounded after him as he drove off, and looking round he saw Job take up the slighted piece of work and turn to his forge.

"If he knew that it was to be called for again to-day, I suppose he would let it alone," thought the young man, laughing. "He hopes to be able to tell the parson that it has been ready and waiting a long time. Well, his bright hopes are doomed to disappointment. Get along, old horse! dinner is ready." And Nahum quickened his pace, scenting his oats from afar.

CHAPTER VI.

ROBIN was standing at her pantry window when Conrad drove into the dooryard and up to the hitching-post. She shook her head at him in merry reproof as he came toward her.

"Late to dinner, Mr. Faulkner! Mrs. Bloom has been sighing like a furnace over her fresh biscuit."

"Don't mention furnaces, I beg of you!" said Conrad, fanning himself with his Panama. "How do you always manage to look so provokingly cool and comfortable?" And he ran an approving eye over the pretty cambric dress she wore.

"Because I have n't time to think of the heat, perhaps," laughed Robin. "Besides, one must be cool in order to make pastry. Look at that!"

"That" was a delicious pile, some six

inches high, composed of thin rounds of the flakiest, most delicate piecrust interlaid with crimson strawberries, and powdered with shining sugar. Over the whole she proceeded now to pour a flood of yellow cream; and held the glass dish, with its aggravating contents, up for Conrad's inspection.

"I trust you have brought home an appetite," she said, gayly, leading the way to the dining-room.

"No need. It is quite capable of creating one for itself.

"And if your appetite should fail (as fail full well it may,
For never saw I promise yet of such a wilting day),
Press where you see this short-cake shine, along the entry
 bobbin',
And be your cynosure to-day the pastry of Miss Robin!"

"Well done!" laughed Robin. "I would clap my hands, only in that case the standard would fall. You will surely be hungry after that effort. I hope so at all events, for I have given you a cold dinner to-day."

"Any other would be out of place. It is perfect. I'll be down directly." And, rushing up to his room, he was back again by the time Mrs. Bloom appeared to pour the water.

Hungry or not, it was a wondrously pleasant meal to the young man. Robin looked as if it were not unpleasant to her. There being but two of them, the usual oval of the table had been reduced to a round, and pushed into the coolest, shadiest corner of the large room. Robin could best have told why the fresh white cloth had been put on to-day, rather than to-morrow, as Mrs. Bloom's good old Sabbath habit was. And why the customary plain goblets had been superseded by dainty, star-cut glasses matching the bubble-like decanter, which had held fiery old Burgundy in grandmother Cary's day, but was now innocent of aught stronger than lemonade. A cluster of nasturtiums, scarlet, gold, and bronze, made the centre of the table gay; and the shortcake was ably flanked by a cold chicken on the one side, and a plate of puffy rolls, over which Mrs. Bloom had certainly sighed to some purpose, on the other; while crisp, cool lettuce, with its dressing in a queer little pitcher beside it, threw an air of refreshment over the whole.

"Launcelot Owen would have written a poem upon such a scene as this," said Conrad, carving the chicken with outward sedateness, but great interior exultation. It was so wonderful to be sitting at table with Robin opposite, and no one else near. For the moment it was almost as if the table were his own — and hers !

" Then you found him."

" I found him. But the fact might have remained forever unknown to me had your uncle not called my attention to it. I was leaning casually against the stone, feeling after an idea that hovered about me like a mosquito, just out of reach. It struck me afterwards that perhaps that particular spot might be a favorite hovering place for such winged gentry."

" Not at all unlikely. That the man had the soul of a poet, I shall always maintain. Some of his verses have the true ring. We will ransack the Cleppitts' library for his old manuscripts some day. I have found one or two blank books half written through already."

" Can you recall any of the sentiments therein contained ? "

" I have copies of several, and there are one or two which have stayed by me of their own accord. Notably, eight short lines to a toad."

" Toads and salad go well together," said

Conrad, handing her a plateful of the cool, curling leaves and proceeding to help himself. "Can't I have him now?"

So, while he cut and dressed his lettuce, Robin repeated : —

> "Thou repulsive, squat-backed toad
> Fatly hopping in my road!
> Shall I hurl thee from the way,
> With rough foot, or let thee stay?
> Haply thou may'st find me too
> Not a handsome thing to view.
> Poor soft wretch! I 'll let thee be.
> God made toads, and God made me."

"Fatly hopping!" quoted Conrad, with fork poised in air. "I can see that toad. Yes, we must rummage the Cleppitt library. I want Launcelot. He is unique. Can't you tell me more about him?"

"Yes, a good deal. I have hunted him up pretty thoroughly, through family records and Miss Doris's memory. To begin with, he was a Welshman. I suppose Uncle Ike has given you some idea of people and things at the Clearing. How it was settled, and so forth."

"He told me a little."

"Well, to give you ' the heads ' as they say hereabouts : When Arthur Cleppitt and his wife came over in 1795, they left behind them, among other friends, Mrs. Cleppitt's brother, Launcelot Owen. And it was pretty well understood in the family that he was only to remain behind long enough to give the girl he was engaged to time for making up her mind and her clothes to emigrate to America with him. The clothes got made, but I fancy material fell short in the other direction, for one day in the following spring Launcelot walked in upon them at the Clearing all alone. He had grown old and thin and grave since they parted from him, but not a word would he say as to what had changed either himself or his prospects. Only, in the course of the year, among other news from Wales, came the tidings of the girl's marriage to another man, a friend of Launcelot's, who had grown up with him from boyhood.

" For fifteen years Mr. Owen lived on with his sister and her husband ; a hard-working, studious, silent man. Children and animals found a loving, tender friend in him. From people in general he kept aloof, except when his ready quill or skillful hands could render any one a service. But the service was always given with few words. Letters from home he would never read nor hear read, and the children were bidden to hold their tongues upon all such topics. At last he died, from a sickness brought on by jumping into the mill-pond in mid-winter to save a poor old dog. The last thing he did was to write his own epitaph, which you have seen."

"I shall see it in a new light next time. Poor fellow! fifteen years of living alone in a crowd. For doubtless a man who was black and blue all over would find even half a dozen whole-bodied neighbors sadly oppressive."

"It might have been worse," remarked Robin, severely dry; "he might have married Celia Jane. When you have read his journals, and bits of things, as I have, you will wonder what manner of creature she could have been to give him up."

"I don't want ter hurry ye a mite, but this is circle afternoon, an' it 's goin' on two o'clock. I 've peeked in twice afore, but ye seemed so kinder contented I hated ter disturb ye."

Conrad laughed, and Robin grew a shade rosier. "It is all my fault, Mrs. Bloom!" exclaimed the former. "I plead guilty to being the only contented one. Miss Robin cannot be, of course, for she has not had any dinner. Let me give you another bit of chicken, and some of the salad," he entreated, turning to Robin as the housekeeper departed in triumph, with her hands full of plates, knives, and forks.

" No, thank you. I have had an ample sufficiency, as Mrs. Bloom would say. You may have all these things," she added to that reëntering worthy. " I want Mr. Faulkner's exclusive attention for this shortcake."

The shortcake and its maker had the young man's exclusive attention for the remainder of the meal, and it must be confessed that the one, in its own peculiar way, deserved it quite as much as the other.

CHAPTER VII.

" ARE you very busy, Mr. Faulkner ? "

" Not a bit," returned Conrad with alacrity, laying aside his pen, and springing up to meet Robin, who at that moment entered the room, dressed in her tramping suit of blue and green plaid. The hat, with its gleaming peacock's breast, hanging from one hand, and a grandmotherly little brown wicker basket in the other.

" This library is a pleasant place, but out of doors is pleasanter. Where are we bound for this time ? "

" I think I won't tell you much about it beyond advising you to bring your letters with you, if they are finished, to put your sketch-book into your pocket, and to prepare yourself for taking notes."

" All of which, being translated, means

that we are bound for the post-office : and
that on one side or the other of that point
you will introduce me to some fresh aspects
of nature, animate and inanimate. I would
give a pretty penny for a glimpse at *your*
mental notes, Miss Robin. You have a keen
eye for character which would be invaluable
to an author."

"And am I not giving an author the benefit of it ? " she retorted gayly, as she put on
her hat and turned away.

"Which reminds me," said Conrad,
gathering up sketch-book and letters, and
following, " that I completed the third
chapter of my story this morning. Suppose
you were to look it over, some time when you
have nothing better to do, and give me your
opinion."

"Suppose I were," assented Robin, nodding her head sagely, to hide the quick flash
of pleasure in her eyes, "and suppose," she
added, half mischievously. half in earnest, — "suppose I should n't like it. How
very awkward that would be ! "

"Not at all. Nothing is ever awkward
between friends, you know. If you do not
like it, you will simply tell me so, and I
shall " —

"Alter it? Oh, no, you won't! because " —

" Well ? "

" Because you are a man, you know. Uncle Ike often asks my advice about his sermons ; but he never takes it — never."

" I shall take it," said Conrad, quietly. " I shall take this enormous basket, too." And he skillfully abstracted it from her hand as he spoke.

" But you must not take that path or we shall part company. I am going this way."

" This way " meant a precipitous plunge down a rough, stony bank at the left, into a meandering and heavily shaded foot-path, which, after they had patiently unraveled its twistings for a quarter of a mile, brought them, by an abrupt and bewildering turn, face to face with the river.

" Here is a mystery ! " exclaimed Conrad, eying with much surprise the little green boat that floated in the shadow of a huge rock to which it was moored. " How have I been in Ockley so long and never discovered this Snug Harbor ? "

" Oh, Ockley abounds in mysteries," replied Robin, enjoying his astonishment. " There are one or two still remaining for you to fathom. If you are very good indeed I may spoil another for you before we get home. Uncle Ike told me to entertain you while he was gone, you know, and he won't be back before nine or ten o'clock."

"I will be good, — very good. But how shall I begin?"

"By letting me row you down, and — would you mind holding the basket right side up? because I don't believe it can improve cup-custards to stand on their heads."

"Your stern command shall be obeyed," said Conrad, seating himself obediently beside the tiller when he had drawn the little craft to the bank, handed Robin in, and pushed off again. "But my heart misgives me in regard to the cup-custards! I supposed they were flowers. Had n't you better — interview them, and find out just where they do stand?"

"You may, if you like," said Robin, gathering an oar into either hand. And as she spoke, she brought her boat's head dexterously about, and began to row down-stream with a slow, steady dip of the oars that told of long experience. She watched, with a little amused smile, while Conrad, handling the basket with great respect now, proceeded to unfasten and raise the cover, and peep under the white, fringed napkin.

" What cups ! " was all he said. And then he quietly replaced the napkin and closed the basket.

" Cups ! " echoed Robin, " are the custards nowhere then ? "

" The custards are all right ; that is, I suppose they are. But the cups are regularly eerie. And so are those slices of golden foam. Witches' fare, I call it. Are you a witch, Miss Robin ? "

" I can make sponge cake."

" Can you ? then no one else can. I fancied I had seen sponge cake before, but I never have. Are we on our way to a picnic, please ? "

" No. We are on our way to Janet."

" And what, or who, is Janet ? if I may ask. Is *she* the witch ? "

" She is two or three things."

" That settles the question beyond a doubt. The description corresponds with the cups. It also accounts for the appetite."

" Appetite ? Oh, you mean the supply is large, I suppose. Janet has two mouths to feed."

" Horrible ! And does one mouth require

custard, while the other craves sponge cake ? ”

Robin’s merry laugh went ringing up the river.

“ One mouth is hers,” she said, demurely, “ the other Cy’s.”

“ Sighs ? over such cake as that ? Clearly this Janet is an undeserving character. I ’ve a mind to eat it myself.”

“ Better not. It ’s eerie. you know. You might get bewitched.”

“ True,” assented Conrad, gravely, though there was a queer look at the corners of his mouth. “ There is danger, I believe. Janet shall have her own.” And placing the basket carefully under the seat as if to remove as far as possible all danger of witchcraft. he took off his hat and settled himself comfortably back in the stern, his eyes wandering from point to point along the river-bank, and coming back frequently to rest for a brief instant upon the graceful, girlish figure before him.

They rounded a curve, and came into deeper water. Under the shadow of the bank it looked black and cool. and the trees bent over till they fairly trailed their long, drooping branches in the stream. In and out

among the shadows darted slim river-fish —
noiseless gray presences, with vacuous eyes.
Robin drew in her oars, and they floated, silently, with the current.

Suddenly, as the boat drifted in, more and
more, toward the shore, Conrad rose to his
feet and made a hasty clutch at one of the
great gray rocks above them. The clutch
accomplished nothing, however, save a vio-
lent rocking of the boat, and the imminent
danger of a cold plunge for himself.

"I beg your pardon!" he exclaimed, with
a rueful, backward glance. "I had no
thought of making such a commotion.
There was something in that cleft of rock
that I wanted — and did n't get."

"So I perceive," said Robin, with her
eyes upon the one wild columbine that still
made a scarlet glow of color against the
rock's rough background. "Next time you
will do well to try for one lower down.
There is a whole clump of them within easy
reach!" and she pulled her left oar to bring
his end of the boat nearer. Conrad laid his
hand upon the oar before she could repeat
the stroke.

"Thank you," he said, quietly, "but if I
cannot have the one I want, I won't have
any."

Robin looked a trifle surprised. This was a phase of character which her friend had never manifested before. He smiled a little as he caught the look.

"Do you believe in omens?"

A quick, questioning glance was her only answer.

"I hung an omen round the stem of that columbine, and wanted to make sure of it. The attempt was a failure, as you saw."

Robin's eyes went back to the speck, growing rapidly fainter in the distance.

"What shall I do about it?" pursued Conrad, gravely, watching her face as she watched the flower.

"If I were you" — she paused.

"Well," a smile at something in his own thoughts lightening the gravity, "let us suppose that impossibility accomplished, — what then?"

"I would take the omen off again."

"But that is impossible."

"Then — is it something you want very much?"

The smile faded, and a deep earnestness came into his voice.

"Very much. More than I ever wanted anything in my life before."

The dark eyes fell before his steady gaze, and the cheeks below them took on a faint reflection of the columbine's vivid color.

The boat had emerged into a sunny stretch now, and the oars began to rise and fall again with measured rhythm. Just ahead appeared the village bridge, with its cluster of stores at one end, and the white steeple at the other. Robin began to pull her left oar again, and the boat drew in to the bank.

Conrad leaped out as the keel grated on the stones, and reached a helping hand to his companion.

"Then" — he repeated, looking straight into her face as she laid down the oars and rose to her feet.

But when Robin was once fairly brought to bay she never flinched. She raised her eyes, and looked as straightly, and more composedly, at him.

"Then — I would have the columbine!"

And just touching his extended hand, she sprang lightly past him and led the way up the bank into the village street.

Just across the bridge, and beyond the church, there was a sudden rise of ground heavily shaded with sugar-maples of massive growth, and fringed along its edges with lusty sumach bushes and close - growing brakes. A narrow foot-path had managed to worm its way through these stout defenders of the height above, and showed its contrasting line of earth-color, only to be instantly lost to view again in the dust of the street it sought. To this point, when the letters had been duly delivered into the official hands of Mr. Bly, Robin led the way. Once there, she paused, provokingly.

"Where do you suppose it leads to?" she asked, with a mischievous smile.

"Beyond the fact that it leads, eventually, to the abode of Cy's grandmother I am at a loss. To tell the truth there has always seemed something so charmingly hidden and mysterious about it that I have hesitated to break the spell by exploring."

"Did n't I tell you that I should spoil another mystery? Come and see!" And bending her head to clear the rather low archway of green, she disappeared in a flash.

Conrad followed, expecting to find himself in the woods, literally as well as figuratively. When lo and behold! the valiant little path, making but one right - angled squirm behind the sheltering sumachs, came to a sudden end at the foot of a flight of irregular stone steps. At their top stood Robin, laughing down at him. She disappeared again, however, and when he reached the uppermost step was nowhere to be seen. Instead he beheld a low-roofed, black cottage; the garden space in front of it gay with hollyhocks, and sunflowers, and clumps of brilliant scarlet sage. The old house was like a phœnix, rising from out its nest of flame. Under a large maple, a little removed, sat an old woman, with her back toward him, spinning. Her white cap, the scant folds of her dull-tinted stuff gown, and the quaint, carved outlines of her age-darkened wheel stood out from the glowing background of color like some old, old picture.

Involuntarily the keen artist-look came into Conrad's eyes, and his hand sought the pocket where his sketch-book lay in ambush. Some one, who had been also lying in ambush, came up, softly, beside him.

"I told you you would want your sketch-book!" cried Robin, in a triumphant whisper.

"Only keep her there for ten short minutes!" implored he, in the same tone, "and you shall have the sketch."

"A bargain," said Robin, promptly, and

that he might not have opportunity to re-
pent his promise, she moved quickly away
and was presently standing beside the nim-
ble wheel.

There is a great deal of expression in the
backs of some people's heads. Conrad
knew, by the quick, pleased bobbing of the
white cap, that the face within it was all
alight at sight of the young girl. The wheel
came to a stop for a moment, and the spin-
ner made as though she would have risen,
but Robin laid her hand on the dull-colored
sleeve and said something, smiling. Then
she moved round to the other side, and sat
down on the grass, quite out of the way,
and the old woman nodded, and twirled her
distaff.

Conrad looked, and sketched, and looked
again. To be sure the cap would whisk
about every few minutes, as though its
wearer found it impossible to keep her
eyes from the bright face at her side; and
once in a while the broad shoulders would
shake in sympathy with the clear sweet
laugh that floated up into the tree-tops.
But the wheel whirled merrily round, and
the model sat very still, considering, and
by the time the allotted ten minutes had

stretched themselves to twenty the outlines for a very promising little picture had been secured.

" My friend, Mr Faulkner, Janet," said Robin, rising from her lowly position as Conrad came round to where she sat.

" Mr. Faulkner is vera welcome," said the old woman, quietly, and she again made a motion as if to rise, but again Robin stopped her.

" No, no, Janet, you must just sit still! we did not come to interrupt you. Mr. Faulkner wants to learn to spin."

" I never saw any one spin flax in this country before. It is very pretty work, and it looks easy too," said Conrad.

" Ay, 't is pretty work, as you say, and easy enough too, like many another thing, when a body knows how. But to me 't is not so much the work itsel' as what it brings to mind that makes it lightsome. 'T is my own mother's wheel this, and well I mind how busily she aye kept it whirling. She had need, too, for there were eight of us, lads and lasses, — and never a factory known in those days. By the ingle neuk in winter, or by the burn-side in summer, many 's the long day I 've seen her sit to spin — spin —

spin, — till I got to think no thread fit to use else. And to this day," concluded the old woman proudly, "not a shred of cloth goes to my back but what my own hands make."

Janet's English had, from long usage, so far got the better of her Scotch as to allow the latter to crop out only in occasional words or sentences, which gathered and thickened like hailstones as her interest in the conversation grew, until, at moments of deep excitement, they pelted down fast and furious on the devoted heads of her listeners.

"Janet," said Robin suddenly, bringing her eyes down from the green labyrinth overhead, which they had been dreamily threading during this last long speech, "I am going to put these much enduring custards into the cupboard for you, and then I am going to look for honey. If I find any may I have it?"

"Ay, and welcome, lassie. There 'll be a fine bit comb in the middle hive ; for the bees and I have been of one mind about it, and it hasna been meddled with. But what 's to do with the friend here, shall he go too?"

"No, no! he must stay with you. The

bees would sting him." And with a gay, backward nod from among the riotous hollyhocks, she disappeared in the shadow of the low doorway.

"And what if they sting her?" asked Conrad, following her with a look that was unconsciously wistful. "Is she proof against bees as against all other harmful things?"

What a keen glance bent itself upon him from under those heavy, gray brows! The rugged face lit up for a brief moment, and then the wonted look of quiet impenetrability drew over it again, like a veil.

"Ay, she's that!" said Janet, quietly; "proof against the devil and all his works. Not that my bees, bonny creatures, have anything in common with him. But sin' ye read her so well," she added abruptly, "step yonder, to the chink in the bushes, and take a peep. It's no' every one I'd be giving the privileege. An' now we'll see what like man he is;" she said to herself, as he thanked her with a smile, and walked away in the direction indicated. "If he be what I think him he'll scarce stand long to glower like a — Na, na! he's ta'en his peep an' come away, like a gentleman. Weel,

Mr. Faulkner, ye're a painter they tell me; what like a picture is yon, think you?"

"Like none that I ever saw before I came to Ockley. I have seen a good many such since."

"Ay, the Lord is a gran' artist! Heard ye ever Miss Robin sing?"

"Never. I have heard her play."

"Ah, her songs are not for all. But to my min', them that have heard her will never hear aught so sweet again, till they hear the angels. Heard ye ever her scold?"

He smiled, quietly, and instantly grew grave again. "I cannot imagine Miss Robin scolding," he said, with a touch of dignity.

Again the light flashed into the old woman's face. But this time it lingered. She ceased her work, and pushing the idle wheel from her looked up into his face with earnest eyes.

"From the time Miss Robin lay in my lap, a bit baby, till this day, no living being ever heard a cross word from her lips. An' yet she's a fine high spirit, like all the Carys. Ah, she's proud! but never too proud to know when she's i' the wrong, an' own to 't. Doubtless, though," she added, suddenly, with a shrewd glance at his half averted face, "doubtless I weary you with all this. It 's an old nurse's nonsense, sir."

He turned to her, from some thought of his own, it seemed.

" Is it ? " was all he said; but the bright, approving smile filled out the meagre sentence. Just at this moment the subject of conversation made her appearance again, carrying a plate. The plate itself was of common ware, but gay with all the flowers that never grew, and upon it reposed a heavy and perfect white comb filled with its treasure of golden honey. The fragrance of whole acres of clover distilled itself upon the summer air as Robin passed along.

" I had to steal a plate, Janet, because it would n't go into the basket without breaking; and besides, paper won't hold it. Did you ever smell anything more delicious in your life ? Talk of greenhouses ! "

" Shall I carry it ? " asked Conrad, after an admiring survey.

" No, indeed ! I must carry it myself. You will have to do the rowing this time, if you don't mind."

" I do mind, always. I minded coming

down, and I shall mind going back. Did n't
I promise to be good?"

"Ah, it's easy to be good with such a re-
ward before one's eyes! is n't it, Janet?"
said Robin, with a laughing look at them,
and an appreciative one at her honeycomb.

"Ay, wonderful easy!" quoth Janet,
dryly; but her look rested higher than the
painted plate. "Come again, Mr. Faulkner,
when it pleases. Any friend o' Miss Robin
is aye welcome here, to say nothing o' Cy.
Ye 've been vera kind to Cy, poor fellow,
he 's never wearied telling about it."

"Cy has been very kind to me. We are
fast friends."

"Cy's friendship will do ye no harm.
Though it 's few would take the trouble to
fin' that out. He 's no such a fool as folk
would make him."

"And that reminds me, Janet, we want
Cy to help us find some trout-pools to-
morrow. We are going over beyond Sage's
hill. Will you tell him, please? Mr. Faulkner, I really cannot wait for you to get all
those hollyhocks by heart! Janet will let
you come another time to sketch."

"'Deed will I! an' stay as long as he
pleases. I 'll not forget to tell Cy, Miss

Robin. If there's any one can fin' the trout for you, he can, an' he'll be gey blithe to get the chance."

"Ay, but they're the bonny pair!" she muttered to herself, as Conrad preceded Robin down the steps and held the boughs aside for her to pass. "He's none too lavish wi' his words, but his deeds seem aye ready enough. An' when the tongue bides, the eyes can work the better. It's few o' her looks an' needs he lets go by him. I doubt he's nigh fitting even for her, an' that's what I never thought to see in this world, after my experience o' the men! One thing I know," and there was a shrewd light in the deep-set eyes, and a kindly curl to the puckered lips, "if he lives to be a cent'ry old he'll never forget the glint he got o' her through old Janet's hedge, stan'in' there wi' the sunshine on her hair an' the flowers at her feet, an' the bonny brown bees flying all about her!"

CHAPTER VIII.

CONRAD rowed slowly up the river in the warm afternoon sunshine, and watched Robin, who, cosily ensconced in his old place at the stern, was watching in her turn the cloud shadows, as they glided noiselessly from base to summit of the nearer hills, the alternate light and shade gleaming over the rugged slopes like sweet, sudden smiles over old, weather-beaten faces, and lazily trailing one hand through the cool, dark water that each stroke of the oars sent rippling shoreward. She came back presently, with a long breath, to find his eyes resting intently upon her.

"How many miles of journeying does that sigh stand for?" he asked.

"To tell the truth, I hardly know my-

self," she answered, lightly. "Somehow
the river always makes me absent-minded.
Handling the oars is the only thing that can
ever keep me from drifting. It is very
stupid of me, I know."

"I beg your pardon," said Conrad, smiling, "I never said so. I do not find your
drifting at all unsociable. Besides, we were
both drifting, I believe."

"Have you ever seen the sunset from that
high ridge beyond the sugar-house?" asked
Robin, rather abruptly.

"How should I? You have never shown
it to me."

"As if sunsets waited for a showman! I
thought you might have been there with Cy,
perhaps."

"No, Cy is not so airy in his movements
as some people. I have had reason to
think that he rather eschews rising ground.
He took me three miles round, the other
day, to avoid crossing Langley Hill. So the
top of the ridge is where you have just come
from!"

"Not exactly. But I have been wondering whether or no you would like to go there.
There will be a glorious sunset to-night.
You see I must keep you amused, somehow,
till Uncle Ike gets back, and " —

"And as you find it an extremely laborious task, you think of coaxing heaven and earth to help you out! Truly I am complimented."

"'Trust a man,' as Mrs. Bloom says, 'to twist everything to his own advantage!'" laughed Robin. "But will you go?"

"Certainly I will. I must be amused, as you say."

"Then we will have tea early, so as to get to the top 'beforehand,' to quote Mrs. Bloom's remarks again."

"Mrs. Bloom is a remarkable woman. But if we are to perform such an unheard of paradox I must do my part." And the oars began to describe such powerful arcs as sent the little boat fairly flying homeward, upstream though it was.

Although tea was a full hour earlier than usual that night, perhaps no more striking example could be found of the rapid degeneration of the human race since the days of Sparta's greatness than the avidity with which this strongly - built and muscular young man fell upon sponge-cake and honey! To tell how many cups of tea he drank, merely for the pleasure of seeing it poured out, would be a most unhandsome piece of treachery. Be it only recorded, then, to his lasting credit and renown, that he wanted another dreadfully, but did not ask for it.

The shadows were slanting longer and longer across the green door-yard as the two young people once more sallied forth, and down the lane, past brook and sugar-house, to where the pasture land began to hump itself up preparatory to forming the high shoulder known as the Ridge.

Mrs. Bloom, carrying cups and saucers, teapot and plates, walked thoughtfully to and fro between dining-room and kitchen, casting now and again a keen glance after the retreating figures, and finally came to a stand-still before the cooking stove.

"H'm!" she ejaculated, nodding her head sagely at the big black kettle, which was steaming away within two feet of her nose; "mebbe they think I can't see a thing like that when it's right afore my eyes!" Which somewhat peculiar remark appeared to relieve her mind to such an extent that she roused up, and went to work with a will; leaving a solitary plate, cup, and saucer in readiness for the parson when he should return to his belated meal.

Meanwhile the two whose affairs occupied

so prominent a place in the worthy housekeeper's thoughts went on and up, all un-
mindful of the interest they were exciting,
till the belt of sugar-maples that skirted the
slope gave way to pines, and the pines in
their turn dwindled and thinned to clumps
of sweet fern and spires of mullein, and they
came out finally upon the bare, rocky crest
just as the sun began to dip down behind
that particular far blue peak which, at this
season, he was wont to make his point of
disappearance.

"There!" exclaimed Robin, sinking down
against a warm wall of rock with a sigh of intense satisfaction. "What did I tell you?"

"Not half," returned Conrad, ungrate-
fully, gazing eagerly forth upon the heav-
ing sea of hills that rolled its giant billows
round about them on every side. "Who
could suppose that a little climb like that
would open out to one such a panorama?
Is n't that the Camel's Hump, over there to
the right?"

"Yes. And there's Monadnock, and
there's Ascutney, and there's — oh, look!
quick! quick! there he goes. Now watch!"
They watched, and watched, while the clouds
above and before them glowed rosy, and

golden, and brown, and died away, like heavenly bonfires, to ashes of sombre gray. The shadows darkened and deepened in the valleys and mountain - clefts, and crept, and crept, and grew until all nature seemed wrapped in dusky twilight as in a veil. Then up, over the eastern hills, in her triumphal, unimpeded progress rose the moon, full-orbed and radiant. They turned their faces from the west, as from a royal death-bed, and offered, courtier-like, their fealty and admiration to the fair queen whose reign was just beginning.

Down, down from the illuminated hill-top where they stood, rolled the gracious, growing light, till it spread itself like a silvery mist over the dark sea of pines below them.

Robin gathered her white shawl closer about her shoulders, and turned slowly and reluctantly to go.

"Miss Robin, just one moment! There can never be so perfect an hour as this again. Won't you sing for me?"

His hand rested lightly on her arm to stay her going, his look rested on her face with eager questioning. In his thoughts Janet's words were repeating themselves. "Ah, her songs are not for all!" Would they be for him?

At his words a little wondering smile had crept over Robin's face. A smile with a question in it, as if she would ask how he had so suddenly discovered that she *could* sing. But she said nothing, only, after a moment's pause, let her arms drop from their folding, and hang, with the hands loosely clasped, before her as she stood leaning lightly against the huge gray bowlder, her face turned to the eastern sky, and the white summer moonlight falling all over and about her. Then, quietly, she began to sing.

Conrad, drawn back into a dark corner the better to see and hear her, fairly held his breath as the full, slow notes rolled forth upon the stillness. There was no noise in Robin's singing. The sweet, rich voice deepened and swelled, or sank to softest modulations; yet at its strongest there was ever a strength reserved, at its faintest it was ever pure and clear.

What that first song was Conrad never could remember. The glorious tones themselves so filled heart and ear as to leave no consciousness of any words. Perfect silence filled the pause after the last deep. velvety notes. She waited a moment and sang again, this time from " Elijah." "Oh. rest in the Lord ! "

Still silence.

Then the thrilling tones were poured forth once more in the beautiful Invocation from the " Magic Flute."

Robin was just a little surprised when the third pause brought still no word from her one listener, sitting far back in the shadow. She broke the silence herself.

" You asked for one song, Mr. Faulkner, and I have sung you three. Are you satisfied ? "

" No ! " he answered, coming forward to her side again ; " but I do not know how to thank you, and I shall never forget it." And as she looked up at him, in the moonlight, she saw that there were tears in his eyes.

They stood, a moment longer, looking out over the boundless expanse of glorified darkness. Then Robin once more gathered her shawl about her, and turning, they left the hour and its beauty behind them forever, and made their way, silently, down the steep decline and through the bare, deserted pasture, to the house again.

When they reached the porch, the usual evening rendezvous, old Nahum was already to be seen making his crab-like way up

the hill. They stood and watched him, or
thought they did.

“This has been a beautiful day,” said
Conrad, slowly.

“Lovely. And to-morrow will be just
such another. The very most perfect weather
for our tramp.”

“I was not thinking of the weather so
much, though it could hardly be finer, as
you say. But I am willing to accept your
prophecy for to-morrow on both grounds.”

“I am glad if to-day has passed pleasantly with you,” said Robin, demurely. “It
relieves my mind of a great burden to hear
you say so. Uncle Ike will be sure to ask.
I know he felt rather shaky as to my entertaining abilities.”

“It has been hardly a fair trial of them,
after all. You had Janet and the moon to
help you,” retorted Conrad, mischievously.

“Janet is a traitor! She told you about
my singing.”

“She told me that you did not sing for
every one, and so ” —

“And so you thought you would try how
much I would do for you!” exclaimed
Robin, half indignantly. “Well, I hope
the result was sufficiently flattering!”

"You sang for me, and sang divinely! I shall always remember that."

There was an earnest ring to his words in which mingled no smallest trace of self-gratulation.

"Do!" said Robin, proudly, "and remember also, that when I promised to be your friend such experiments became unnecessary. Had you told me plainly why you wanted a song, you should have had it, all the same."

"I believe you!" he answered, warmly, "for you are unlike all other women whom I have ever met."

"You must have met some delightful people," said Robin, her momentary displeasure losing itself in amusement, "if I am the first of your acquaintance who has ever told the truth!"

"Ah! but then they have almost all been delightfully amiable. Whereas I hear that you" —

"Go on."

"Have a quick temper, and are most inordinately proud."

Such a ringing, joyous laugh as went floating out into the moonlight! In its merry waves the creaking of the old chaise, as it drew up before the door, was almost drowned.

"Oh ho! Some one seems to feel rather jolly," exclaimed the parson. "Guess you have n't missed me much, after all. Whoa, Nahum!"

"Miss Robin was making merry over her own shortcomings, sir," said Conrad, hastening down the steps to assist his host. "*I* have missed you terribly."

"I 'll warrant it!" chuckled the parson, descending cautiously, as became old bones, from his rather tottery perch. "She is a terribly tiresome kind of girl. How much country has she dragged you over to-day?"

"'Quite a piece,' as Abijah definitely remarks. I have been numbered among 'all who travel by land or by water.' However, I have borne it fairly well. Let me take those things." And he proceeded to rob the venerable gentleman of kerosene can and molasses jug, not omitting to secure also, from beneath the seat of the chaise, the gay calico mail-bag, a marvel of construction, inaugurated by Mrs. Bloom, "ter pervent mistakes."

"That feller Bly is forever a blunderin' an' chargin' it to other folks. We 'll hev a bag; and then, ef there *is* a mess made, why there can't be no backin' aout." So the mail-bag, with its jolly yellow palm-leaves on a brick-red ground, came to be an institution in the neighborhood, and nightly swelled or shrunk like fancy stocks as the case might be. It was very fat to-night. Conrad patted its buxom sides affectionately as he gave it into Robin's outstretched hands. Then he passed on through the dining-room where the parson was already making progress with his tea, and delivering can and jug into the tender keeping of Mrs. Bloom, completed the circle of his usefulness by way of the back-door and the grass-plot, and so came round once more to where Robin sat on the steps.

"Only one letter — for Uncle Ike. The rest was all newspapers."

"So much the better. We can forego the luxury of a kerosene lamp. How moonlight rests one."

"One kerosene lamp?"

"One burning and shining light like myself. Do you know I feel as though we had accomplished a great deal to-day. And yet, there remains one thing more to be accomplished before I sleep!"

"Better accomplish it quickly, then, if you have any idea of a nap to-night. Do you know what time it is?"

"Is it nine?"

"No, it is ten. The clock has just struck. Shall I get the lamp for you, after all?"

"Moonlight will be quite sufficient, thank you."

"To write by?" asked Robin, rising to her feet with a puzzled look.

"To take your advice by."

"What *do* you mean?"

"I mean to have that columbine, or perish in the attempt. Good-night, dear friend!"

CHAPTER IX.

LETITIA LANDON.

WHETHER the Saturday's walks, or the Monday's fishing, or both were to blame for it, Robin could not tell ; but she woke on Tuesday morning with a hard headache, which made her glad to lay her head back speedily on the pillow, and forbade her attempting to rise.

" She 'll keep her bed to-day, anyhow," summed up Mrs. Bloom, making her unwelcome announcement in the breakfast room ; " an' I ruther guess ter - morrer. An' ef she 's so 's ter be up a Thursd'y I sh'll be agree'bly disapp'inted."

So the two gentlemen poured tea and coffee for themselves, helped to their own soup and pudding, worried a good deal inside while making strenuous efforts to appear jolly outwardly, and were generally miserable; although, to a casual observer, they would doubtless have presented quite a cosy and comfortable appearance.

The parson could relieve his mind by occasional audible outbursts; but after the first expressions of concern on Conrad's part nothing further seemed called for from him beyond occasional inquiry. So he was fain to bottle up his real anxiety and wait, with what patience he might, for further developments.

A long tramp, some letter-writing, and various talks with the parson finally disposed of the time between breakfast and tea; and by dint of going to bed two hours earlier than usual he managed to get rid of the evening. But the inexorable moment arrived at length when he must open his eyes again, and face another day without Robin. An anxious man is apt to be a most miserable animal, and our friend proved himself no exception to the general rule. To increase his discomfort the parson, after a visit to his niece's room and many apologies to his guest for leaving him so entirely to himself, departed on business which would detain him for the greater part of the day, and which could not be postponed. Conrad watched him drive away, and then retreated to the library where he read a little, wrote a little, walked up and down a little, and yawned a good deal; until shrewd Mrs. Bloom, divining the state of things, advanced boldly to the rescue.

"Mr. Forkner," she said, pausing at the door on her way upstairs with a glass of water for her patient, "the parson he won't be back afore night an' Miss Robin needs all my time an' trottin'. Now here's Cy stayed here last night an' hain't an earthly thing ter do. Why don't you an' him go off sumw'ers a-fishin', or a-froggin', or a-picter-makin' an' leave the house clear an' quiet? I'll put ye up the best cold dinner in Ockley; but I declare for 't I don't see how I'm ever ter git a hot one, this day."

" But," said Conrad, looking relieved in spite of himself at this energetic proposal, " Abijah has gone with Mr. Carey. What will you do, with no one in the house, in case you want to send to the village?"

" Shan't want ter. I've got as many bottles in my clusset as Mister Lunt has in his

hull shop.   Moreover, ef I do, I 'll collar
one o' them Choat boys.   Ye 'd a sight better go, it 'll do ye more good ter stay out
doors than ter mull in this here liberry all
day.   Besides, ter tell the trewth, an' the
hull trewth, an' nothin' *but* the trewth, I 'd
ruther hev ye out o' my way than in it!   A
man 's dredfully underfoot when there 's
sickness in a house.   I don't mind sayin' I
should feel relieved ef you was out of it."

"I see you would," his gravity fairly giving way before this ingenuous outburst;
"and I will get out of it as speedily as possible.   But tell me, Mrs. Bloom," he demanded, the shadow creeping back deeper
than before; "do you think she is going to
be very ill?"

"Can't tell, yet," returned the housekeeper importantly, making her features as
wooden and inscrutable as possible; "depends on Providence.   I know one thing,
though, my standin' here talkin' won't cure
her!   You just git your traps together an'
I 'll hev my part ready as soon as you be."
And the good woman departed hastily to
administer the glass of water and prepare a
lunch-basket.

When she returned she brought. in addition to the basket, a little roll of manuscript secured by a rubber strap.

" Miss Robin wants I should give ye these. You'll know what they are, she says; an' you're to tell Cy ter take ye over ter Humpy Holler, an' she's very sorry ter be so stewpidly unhorsepittable, — there ! Them ain't my choice o' words," added the housekeeper, with a sigh of relief; " I give ye the message as 't was gi'n ter me. Ye've a right t' express it differ'nt, ef it don't agree with ye."

So Conrad and Cy departed, leaving Mrs. Bloom to the quiet and undivided sway she craved.

" Cy," said Conrad, " we are to proceed, forthwith, to Humpy Hollow. I suppose you know where that is."

Cy grunted; his usual mode of assent. " 'Ts about two mile south o' here ; but it's a hot walk ter git to it."

" I don't mind, if you don't."

" 'Ts nothin' ter me. I 've be'n there hotter days 'n this." So Cy assumed the dinner-basket and they set forth.

Over bare, unshaded pasture lots, along a sandy strip of road, through some bar-places, and across a plowed field, where their shoes got filled with the hot, dry earth and the sun beat down upon them in all his golden fury, they came at last to descend, along a rather precipitous path, into an irregular green basin between the hills, wherein, as if the latter found it hard to stop so suddenly, cropped up various rough hillocks overgrown with birches and cedars, and draped along their rocky sides with hardy, close-clinging little ferns.

"Here 's where Miss Robin alwers sits," remarked Cy, piloting his companion to a rocky nook high up on one of the " humps," whence an extended outlook was to be had through a rift in the bigger hills. " She says she wants that crack ahead ter breathe threw."

" One does get a glorious breath here, that 's a fact," assented Conrad, stretching himself back luxuriously among the fern-cushioned rocks that gathered him into their green embrace. " Does Miss Robin come here often ? "

" Pritty of'n. She brings her sewin', an' plays Titers."

" Plays — Would you mind just saying the name of that game again ? " asked the gentleman, with a bewildered look.

"Titers. She says they're mostly a bad lot, but he's the best of 'em."

"Indeed? Did she ever happen to mention which was the worst?"

"Yes. His name's — well I forgit naow, but he's the feller that fiddled. Come to think on 't he ended up with an ' oh ' ! "

"He ended up easier than he deserved, then, if he is the 'feller' I think him," laughed Conrad, a sudden light breaking upon his groping understanding. "Was it Nero?"

"That's him!" exclaimed Cy, "near-oh! Ye know most everythin', don't ye?" he queried, gazing up into his patron's face with admiring awe.

"Well, there are a few minor points on which I have, as yet, to be enlightened, Cy. For instance, how Miss Robin plays Titus. You have not made it absolutely clear, so to speak. What does she do?"

"Nothin', but sew, an' look at me."

"Neither of which pursuits are, to the best of my memory, accredited to the great Cæsar," murmured Conrad, lazily.

"An' I'm Gladdiater. D'ye know him?"

"He's legion. Yes, I know him. Well, I'll play Titus to-day. Where are the wild beasts?"

" I 'll show ye, if ye 'll wait a minnit!"

Cy's heavy face lighted up; there came a glow into the dull eyes. He was so pleased that he possessed even one accomplishment by means of which he could lay a few amused moments at his friend's feet. He crept softly down where they had climbed up, and Conrad presently saw him come out upon the arena of smooth green turf, fifty feet below, and lay himself flat on his back in the very centre thereof. He made a sufficiently uncouth figure, outstretched in all his physical disproportion in that favored nook where Nature herself had spared no pains, seemingly, to soften and beautify her own harsh outlines. The athletes of ancient Rome would have spurned aside, with rough disdain, such a claimant to membership in their fraternity. But presently, lying there motionless and happy, Cy began a low, monotonous call. Hark! what rustled the dry leaves yonder in the thicket? A brown wood-rabbit poked its nose cautiously from among the lower rocks, and gradually emerged, a second following.

They sat up on their little haunches, sniffing the air inquiringly: but Conrad had the wind in his favor, and his perch was high. Presently, seeing only Cy, to whose presence it would seem they were entirely wonted, the shy feet waxed bolder and brought their owners, with hesitating hops, to where the fat boy lay.

The low call came again. Another and another rabbit deserted its hidden covert and drew near, till some fifteen or twenty, young and old, were hopping and feeding all about him. They came closer, and ate from his hand; while a few of the larger ones even permitted him to stroke their long, thin ears and gently scratch their timid heads.

The sun mounted higher and higher into the heavens, and still Cy played with the rabbits while Conrad looked on. He had managed to draw his sketch-book stealthily from his pocket, and the moments flew by as he endeavored to transfer to paper something of the pretty tableau before him.

The soft, graceful little creatures frisked and feasted to their hearts' content; forming continually new and prettier groupings, so that their unseen portrayer was kept constantly rubbing out and altering, — as his unconscious models tempted him.

But other eyes had sighted the defenseless wild beasts as they fed and frolicked around and over this most gentle gladiator. Cruel, greedy eyes above a ruthless beak. There came a shiver of wind among the birches, the shadow of stealthy, hovering wings fell upon the little grass plot, and a harsh, angry scream rang, echoing, among the hills as Cy scrambled to his feet, brandishing his big straw hat, and every rabbit scurried out of sight in an instant, while the baffled hawk soared slowly away over the tops of the forest trees.

" Is that Domitian ? " queried Conrad, as Cy came up to where he sat, indicating with the butt-end of his pencil the defeated bird of prey now but a dark speck in the distant heavens.

" No, sir," answered Cy, innocently, shading his eyes with his hands the better to follow the creature's circling flight. " That's an old hawk. He's a terrible big feller, — lives over in them woods back o' Cap'n Crehore's. I 've seed his nest."

" All right, Cy, if you 're willing to vouch for him. He made a nuisance of himself so far as I am concerned, though ! " and Conrad glanced ruefully down at his unfinished sketch.

"Be ye makin' a picter o' me?" asked the fat boy, looking over his friend's shoulder and recognizing the various points of resemblance between the half - made sketch and the recently enacted scene.

"I was. It's not finished, — never will be now, I suppose, thanks to Domitian."

"I'm awful humly, ain't I?" pursued Cy, dejectedly, never questioning the likeness to himself in the outlines so hastily thrown upon the page before him. "Why do ye s'pose I be?"

"You're not finished yet either, Cy," replied his friend, in a suspiciously cheery voice, turning toward the spot where the lunch basket reposed; "but you will be, one of these days, by a master hand! That's the difference between you and the picture. Now, then, here are sandwiches, and gingerbread, and pie, and a little of everything! What will you try first?"

They made a capital dinner, — "the best in Ockley" Conrad felt, no doubt, washed down as it was by cold, sparkling water from one of the never-failing rock springs. But for the tenacious little thread of anxiety that bound his thoughts to a certain closed chamber door two miles away, the whole

day's programme would have proved thoroughly enjoyable to him. As it was he
felt a secret drawing toward nearer neighborhood, although, with Mrs. Bloom's characteristic dismissal lingering in his ears, he
dared not present himself before the eyes of
that energetic matron prior to five o'clock,
at the earliest. So he cooked up an alternative.

"Cy, that last piece of cheese was the
touch too much. I believe I have over-
finished my dinner. What do you say to a
little locomotion as an aid to digestion?
Shall we start along homewards?"

Cy understood the last five words and
wisely ignored the preceding ones.

"It's turrible hot, an' I'm turrible full,
— but then the basket's empty."

"You're a philosopher, Cy," laughed
Conrad. "Come along! We will keep in
the edge of the woods, where it is shady,
and when we get to the cascade we will lie
around till tea-time, and I'll read you some
verses."

"Verses" was Greek to Cy, but "lying
around" sounded intelligible and refreshing.
He caught up the empty basket and followed
his leader's brisk example with wonderful
alacrity, considering the "turrible fullness."

It was nearly three o'clock when they came out upon the bank of the brook by the big basin. Cy threw down first the basket, and then himself with a deep grunt of satisfied attainment. It was delightfully cool and shady here, and the clean, pure sound of the running water seemed to wash away from one's mind all memory of dust and fatigue. Conrad cast aside his hat, and leaned contentedly back against the generous trunk of a big beech, his eyes following the steady rush of the brook, his thoughts drifting back, along the stream of time, to that morning when he had first discovered this lovely spot and so much else beside. A glad little current of undefined feeling had been flowing and growing in his life, too, of late. Following it up to its source, as he had the brook, he found that its first leap out into the sunshine had been on that very June morning when the wise men of Gotham had, by the overturning of their own bowl, been the unconscious means of filling his cup of pleasure to the brim. The little current had deepened and broadened with a vengeance of late. The shadows were fast being left behind, and the eager torrent was rushing onward to its final leap

into the glad sunshine of joy, with a song
of thanksgiving? or — Conrad would not
think of that alternative. It looked too
dark and terrible an abysm. He turned
back hastily to the present moment, and
slipped the strap from Robin's roll of papers.

"Look here, Cy! you had first choice of
pie — I 'll take my turn now at the pie-try.
Hark ye, friend!"

CAPRICE.

A sound of dancing footfalls strikes my ear ;
'Mid sombre stems of steadfast woods I catch
The glimmer of a robe all changeable
With palest green that ever fades to gray,
And gray that brightens into palest green.
Around its hem a border, richly wrought,
In fresh, young leaves and blades of springing grass,
With here and there a fair bud peeping out
Of violet, or frail anemone,
Or furry-hooded, shy hepatica.
Above the robe, a wondrous, varying face,
Whose sweet lips smile even while the radiant eyes
Shine tender through a mist of unshed tears.
Over the shoulders, in their supple grace,
Warm-waving hair half hides its deepening gold
Beneath a veil's dull-tinted, envious fold,
Whence the sly air, from stealing through it, gets
A fragrance like the breath of violets.

"I know you, April, with your rainbow mien !
You fooled me last year, can I trust you this ?"
She puts her cool, responsive hand in mine
And breathes bright promises for days to come.

The sunshine falls with kindlier, warmer glow,
Bringing a hint of summer time ; I think —
Fond fool ! — "she will not play me false again."
Then — all at once — the quick eyes fill with tears ;
A moist wind strikes me with a sudden chill ;
The clear green of her garment fades to gray ;
Along the sward the sunlight shimmers pale ;
She softly sighs, and turns her head away,
And round her draws the dull mist of her veil.

It was a thousand pities Robin could not have heard her friend read that poem, for his reading was something to hear. Cy watched his face with half-shut, sleepy eyes. The words were meaningless, or nearly so, to him, but the mellow, musical tones soothed the fat boy's very soul, and he manifested his appreciation by yielding utterly to their power. In other words, he fell asleep.

Conrad glanced at him when the last line was read, and smiled to see the novel effect which his elocutionary powers had produced. Then he went on, reading to himself. There were four poems in all, copied from the originals, all but the old time spelling, in Robin's clear, legible handwriting. The last one held, as Conrad knew, the beginning of a lifetime's bitterness in its two short stanzas.

He had felt from the first a strange attraction, a sort of spiritual kinship to this dead and gone farmer-poet ; and now, from the warmth and gladness of his own sunny present, his heart went out in keen sympathy to the man whose sad history had come to its end so far back in the shadowy past.

ESTRANGED.

The sunset clouds look strangely gray to-night ;
    The evening air blows keen ;
And when I turn to see your window-light
That should have made my homeward path so bright,
    Dark shadows fall between.

A stealthy wind comes creeping from the meres,
    And all the branches moan.
No hand in mine, as in the bygone years ;
With weary heart-ache, and with bitter tears
    I tread my way alone.

Conrad read the few lines over and over. They haunted him somehow. Actually, he was almost beginning to feel as if he were the man who had written them. This would never do! He sat up again, with a quick jerk, and strapped the sheets together. The sun was fast sinking below the tree-tops. He woke Cy, who rolled over and up with a prolonged snore, and set his face and his feet gladly in the homeward way. As he reached the house from one side the parson and Abijah drove up from the other ; they met at the door.

"Better," was Mrs. Bloom's laconic reply to the double fire of inquiry opened upon her a moment later. "Consider'ble better. Havin' the house to herself's done her good, I guess," she added, with an eye - twinkle. "Ef she sleeps good ter-night, mebbe she'll be up an' about ter-morrer."

There was joy depicted upon the two masculine faces before her as the housekeeper told her tale; and the expression of one of them was so unmistakable that the worthy woman could not refrain from remarking to its owner, meeting him, later, on his way upstairs: —

"*Why* Miss Robin did n't up an' hev a fever the Lord knows better 'n I do!" And as she walked off, leaving that flea in his ear, she said to herself: —

"A little scare does 'em a sight o' good. I never *could* see a man a-totterin' on the verge a'thout wantin' ter give him a helpin' poke!"

CHAPTER X.

WHEN Robin came down to a late breakfast next morning no one was visible : but beside her plate stood a little birch-bark basket full of wild raspberries, with a knot of delicate wild flowers and ferns laid lightly on top. For a moment, as she bent over to inhale the rich fragrance, her cheeks reflected the ripe hue of the fruit; but Mrs. Bloom, bustling in with the breakfast tray, soon dispelled all romance.

" There, now you 've seen them things I 'll put 'em inter the refidgerater an' you can hev 'em ter-morrer, ef ye must. The idee o' fetchin' sour fruit to any one that 's jest dodged a fever ! That 's all a man knows."

" I suppose," said Robin, demurely, fastening the flower-cluster in its place among her muslin ruffles as she spoke, — " I suppose Uncle Ike thought I should like them."

" Uncle Ike ! " exclaimed the housekeeper. " You don't s'pose the parson 's be'n pokin' raound amongst the wet grass for that truck ? No, no, Miss Robin ! 't was t' other one. An' he 's gone off ter the village naow, afoot. Guess he thought 't would be the best way ter dry his boots." She was making off with the bark basket when her mistress laid a detaining hand on her calico sleeve.

" Softly, Mrs. B. ! you jump to conclusions. Instead of carrying off my berries just bring me a glass plate, please, and a pitcher of cream. Did you really suppose I should consent to having those lovely things frozen to death in your refrigerator ? "

" Well, no, I can't say I did ! " retorted Mrs. Bloom, slowly relinquishing her prey, and producing the articles called for with a promptitude suspiciously suggestive of their having been ready beforehand. " I 've be'n through the mill three times too of'n ter be sech a fool as ter s'pose any sech a thing. It 's my belief gals would thrive on p'ison, under some circumstarnces ! " And having secured that last word, in which her soul delighted, the jolly old lady departed, chuckling to herself.

Robin poured cream into and over her

pretty crimson thimbles and ate them leisurely and smilingly. If they were sour she
did not discover it, apparently. Then she
took, from the chair into which she had
dropped them, a book and a soft, woolly
shawl and went out to ensconce herself beneath the shade of the biggest elm, where
Conrad, some half hour later, found her.

"Are you a lover of novels, Miss Robin?"
he asked, when he had both looked and
spoken, most emphatically, his pleasure at
seeing her again, and she had thanked him
for the raspberries, and the flowers, which
his eyes had been quick to note in their new
resting-place.

"When I can get time, and a good story,
which, I grieve to say, this is not."

"What is the matter with it? I am in-
terested in such criticisms just now. Not
well written?"

"Oh, very, according to the modern, accepted standard."

"Then what do you object to in it?"

"I object to the standard. You perceive
that my criticism betrays a very uncultured
mind. I do not enjoy clinical literature.
This having every inmost fault and foible
laid bare, every trait and tendency held up,

so to speak, on the point of a scalpel, savors a trifle too strongly of the dissecting-room. In fact, with many modern novelists, as with modern surgeons, the more repellent and abnormal the conditions exposed, the greater glory to the operator. Heroes and heroines used to be interesting people; nowadays they are, mostly, 'beautiful cases.' I feel as if I had been eating 'agates and cantharyds,' and had brought on a fit of indigestion!" And she tossed the offending volume down upon the grass. Then she looked up and laughed. "I am wasting a good deal of moral energy on the old thing! but, seriously, Mr. Faulkner, do put people into your book as you find them, and leave them to speak for themselves. One likes to make friends on paper as one does in reality. Imagine what a pleasant summer we should have been having if there had been one of these character chemists on hand to analyze every word and action, and report!" Her merry laugh rang out again.

"I am no character chemist," warmly returned Conrad, in whose thoughts the particular romance of which himself was the hero was just now occupying first place; "but I have made some discoveries, nevertheless."

"And what might they be, pray?" questioned the girl, innocently, though her color rose.

"A wealth of pure gold, for one thing!" the young man's tones were growing earnest. The eager, rushing torrent threatened to break bounds.

"That must be the butter." She spoke lightly, but her eyes were down, and her own voice a trifle unsteady.

"No, it is not; although I must confess the butter has helped me greatly in my researches. I only wish" —

"Here comes Uncle Ike!" interrupted Robin, rising quickly to her feet as the parson was seen approaching.

Conrad stooped and picked up the discarded novel.

"Miss Robin," he said, speaking quickly and low; "you must not walk to-day, but won't you drive with me this afternoon?"

"Perhaps so, if nothing turns up 'ter pervent,'" returned Robin as hurriedly; making use of the oft-quoted Mrs. Bloom to cover her embarrassment. Then she turned to greet her uncle, who held a yellow envelope in his hand.

"A telegram from Terry, my dear. He

will be at the Falls this afternoon by the 4.30 train. We must all drive over to meet him, if you are able."

"Oh, yes, I am able," answered Robin, slowly; but she sent one quick glance in Conrad's direction as if to say: "Something *has* turned up, you see!"

For him, he felt as if something — creation or his plans, either would produce much the same sensation — had turned over. He went to his room and flung his unopened mail down upon the table. It remained unopened for the rest of the day.

Terry came. His white straw hat, with its broad, blue band, was seen waving from the car-steps as the train swept round the curve; and the quick spring which he made to the platform, the long strides which brought him instantly to the side of the open wagon where his friends sat waiting for him, to say nothing of his beaming face, were evidence enough of his gladness at being there. The parson was sincerely glad to see him too. If there were any of the party whose pleasure at the meeting was qualified, at least they succeeded in concealing the fact. Terry had no cause to complain of his welcome, as he took the seat left for him beside his uncle.

"I tell you what it is, good people, you don't half appreciate your blessings!" he exclaimed, baring his curly head to the mountain breeze as the wagon rolled smoothly along the shaded road. "Just spend one July day where I have spent *thirty*-one, and you will begin to have some idea of the value of this sort of thing. Gracious! it's something like heaven : one five minutes of it pays for so much." And sitting sidewise, the better to take in all his blessings at once, he beamed across at Robin with such infectious happiness that she beamed back again from sheer sympathy.

"How glad she is to see him !" thought the young man who had *not* just arrived. It is strange how ready we all are to judge even our nearest and dearest from the outside. At the very moment too that we are ourselves putting forth strenuous exertions to prevent our own outside from revealing that which seethes within. It occasioned a most unreasonable feeling of discomfort to Conrad that Robin should apparently find it so easy and pleasant to have their own short-lived plan given up, and should have it in her heart to laugh and chat gayly with her cousin as they drove slowly home through the genial summer afternoon. Meanwhile, keeping all these emotions carefully to himself, he laughed, and chatted with them.

Mrs. Bloom was at the door when they drove up, to accord a hearty welcome to the new-comer. Terry was a great favorite with her notwithstanding the " exclimation marks." Time would soften these down into decorous periods soon enough. " Moreover, Miss Robin, ef a boy ain't a *real* boy, he 'll never be a real man ! " So, as in her estimation the young man was not considered to have outgrown his boyhood yet, by any means, she had manifested her satisfaction with his arrival in the old, boyhood way. The table was fairly loaded down with all the good things for which he had formerly been known to express a preference.

" By Jove, Tabby ! " he exclaimed, nicking her scriptural cognomen as no other human being ever dared to do. " you 've killed the fatted calf to - night and no mistake. How is one poor mortal to eat waffles and short-cake and cream-toast all at once ? to say nothing of the fancy articles. I 'll bet Mother Hubbard's cupboard is bare this time ! "

" No 't ain't," contradicted the dame, with

broad delight depicted on her countenance;
"I look out ter hev' it extry full when you
come, Master Terry, alwers.   Eat away!
'ts all good."

"Its goodness is the worst of it," groaned
Terry.   "I always heard that starving people were fed a little at a time, but it seems
they are n't.   Just look at that tumbler of
cream!   Here 's your good health, Tabby."

"Thank Miss Robin fer that, Master
Terry.   She 's a wonderful hand at a dairy.
The butter an' cream she gits out o' them
cows o' hern is somethin' onbelievable, an',
too, Debby Hawkins says she 'd ruther hev
our skim-milk than any other folks's that
hed n't be'n skum."

"She can have it," laughed Terry, always
delighted when he could succeed in betraying
his voluble friend into one of her more striking grammatical lapses. "Cream is good
enough for me.   I 'll take another glass
for breakfast — if I live through the night.
Uncle Ike, how can you insult such richness
by putting tea into it? it 's a sin."

"Oh, Conrad and I are old fogies, and
like our ' cup o' kindness,' " replied the parson.   "Besides," he added, his shrewd
eyes twinkling, " we like to see Robin make
it, you know."

Conrad smiled, quietly, and handed his cup to be refilled. Terry sobered down for a minute and his heart, or his supper, began to weigh a trifle heavy.

"Have you brought your violin, Terry?" asked Robin, glad to turn attention from herself and her tea-tray; "there are one or two things that I want to try over with you."

"There are a dozen that I want to try with you," said Terry, brightening instantly. "Abijah has just brought the traps, suppose we have a little practice before dark."

"Suppose we do," assented the parson; "go and get your tuning up done, Terry, if you are through supper, and we'll come directly. It is a treat, Conrad, I assure you, to hear those two play together." And the parson applied himself to finishing his tea and toast preparatory to a good time.

"A treat," Conrad could not but acknowledge it to be, even though served in a way that was not altogether such as he would have chosen. Often and well as he had heard them each play separately, he was hardly prepared for the perfect command and feeling that blended vibrant piano and quivering violin into what seemed the tone of one transcendent instrument.

"Before dark," Terry had said; but it grew to be long after dark and still the tireless musicians played on, and the charmed audience, swelled to four by the stealing in of Mrs. Bloom and Abijah, listened.

There are at least two distinctly different musical temperaments. One that under the influence of sweet or harmonious sounds grows quieted, soothed, and happy; another that under the self-same conditions becomes excited, intoxicated, electrically charged. When they ceased playing, Robin was sweetly subdued, Terry as nervous as a witch. He laid his violin tenderly away into its little black coffin, and began to pace the shadowy room with hasty strides.

"Terry is letting off steam now," observed Conrad, as Robin came up to where he was sitting in the deep bay-window. "He tears up and down our little room in the city sometimes until I am ready to crawl under the table for safety."

"Music takes hold of him tremendously," replied his cousin, apologetically. "I am afraid we have played too long to-night: but it is always such a temptation to play with Terry."

"There is some temptation about it for him, I take it."

" Yes, we both enjoy ourselves ; we have been accustomed to play together ever since we were children. But indeed," she added, smiling, " we do not always forget other people so rudely as we did this evening. I hope we have not tired anybody."

" Your music could never tire me," answered Conrad, truthfully ; but he did not follow Mrs. Bloom's praiseworthy example of telling " the hull truth ; " he did not say how bitter he found the notion that she could " forget other people," when he happened to be one of them.

Neither did Robin say that she had long since ceased to count him in with " other people " at all. Perhaps she thought he should be acute enough to discover the fact for himself.

CHAPTER XI.

WORDSWORTH.

" MISTER FORKNER ! "

" Well, Cy."

" Is Mister Jacks'n a friend o' yourn ? "

" To be sure he is ; what then ? " replied Conrad, who, seated on his stool in front of Janet's cottage, was working away busily at the sketch he had promised to Robin. It was fast developing from a sketch into a finished picture.

" Nothin', only I was goin' ter say I wisht he had n't ha' come, an' I thought ef he was a friend o' yourn, I would n't."

Conrad laughed ; so did Janet, who was sitting at her wheel and sitting for her picture at the same time.

" Ye 've a proper jeedgement, bairn ! I suspicion 't would be an ill chance for ony one to misliken one o' Maister Faulkner's friends."

" Honest criticism is always allowable,"

said Conrad. "What have you against this particular friend of mine, Cy?"

"Nothin' ag'in *him* as I knows on; I don't like his pistil."

"Ay, ay, I thought as muckle," nodded his grandmother. "Terry Jackson was always rayther a lightsome, careless-spoken callant; but Cyrus never made objection to him till three years syne, afore he went to Germany, ye ken, whan he came up for the summer bringing wi' him his first whisker an' his first fire-arm. From that day to this the lad's been fair crazy wi' appreheension whanever him an' his pistol hae been around."

"Terry is a good shot, Cy, you need not be afraid, he won't hit you."

"It's no for himsel' he's feared," answered Janet for him: "it's just the poor bit beasties he's so fond of. All through the woods an' fields he's his pets an' playthings, an' whan the pistol's by he fair trembles for their lives."

"That is hard. I must confess I sympathize with him too, though I doubt if my influence goes far enough to suppress the revolver entirely. One thing I can promise, Cy," he said, looking kindly upon the anxious fat boy, "when I am with him your friends shall not be hurt, if I can help it."

"Be ye goin' over ter Porter's Pond ter-morrer?"

"Yes, and you are going too. Be sure you are on hand bright and early, Cy. And by the way," here Conrad bent toward him and spoke a few words in a low voice. Cy nodded, and rising heavily to his feet disappeared down the steps. His grandmother followed the slouching figure with misty eyes.

"Maister Faulkner," she said, earnestly, forgetting for a moment to turn her wheel, "none save the Lord an' the boy himsel' will ever fathom what ye 've been to him this twa' month past. Miss Robin 's — weel she 's just Miss Robin, an' ye ken a' *that* means as weel, pretty nigh, as I do mysel' ; but that a gentleman an' a stranger should find aught to companion wi' in such as him has been just a won'erful upleeftin' to the lad. I declare, sometimes it fair 'mazes me to see how changed he is. He 's no half so stupid-like as he used to be. D 'ye know, Maister Faulkner," she added, hurriedly, smoothing her thread idly in her hands and speaking low, — "d 'ye know it sometimes

comes o'er me that he is na' long for this?
It seems as though the Lord was just sendin'
him this bright summer to soften down the
contrast like atween this an' yon." And she
motioned with uplifted hand to the fair blue
arch above them.

"Arguing on those grounds, Janet, there
would be one more, at least, to go. This has
been a bright, bright summer to me too."

"An' may there be mony anither to follow, say I! but there's a mighty differ
atween yoursel' an' Cy. He was born
among the shadows, poor bairn; his sunshine 'll no be o' this warl."

"We seldom know all of each other's
shadows," said Conrad, quietly, deepening
some of those in his picture as he spoke;
"there is only one state of things in which
we are promised the noonday brightness
that knows no shadowing; but the promise
stands. Here every little line of light casts
also its line of shade, but there will be no
dark places there, Janet."

Janet looked at him; a look keen, pitiful,
and satisfied all at once.

"It's true," she said, gravely, while the
soft burr-r of the wheel began afresh, "but
ye're gey young to ha' fund it oot."

If Cy could have peeped into Mr. Jackson's room next morning and seen the preparations which that gentleman was making for the day's excursion, he would hardly have given the happy consent which he did to act as guide on the occasion. He could not peep, however, and Terry, being quite ignorant and innocent on his part of anything unpleasant to others in his proceedings, completed his arrangements satisfactorily to himself, and then walked out into the summer morning, humming as he went that particular duet which he and Robin had last tackled. The sun was just up, the air cool and perfume-y; it was an hour of sweet influences.

Good Mrs. Bloom, stirring briskly about in her big kitchen, felt the influences, though she had no time to stop for them; and there was something of the freshness of the morning in her shrewd, kindly face as she turned, presently, to respond to the familiar greeting spoken over her shoulder from the open door behind.

Terry sat on the broad stone step whipping off yarrow heads with a slender switch. He was apt to have a stick of some sort in his hand; it was a long established habit, dating back to the days when he had wandered over the farm with Robin, boy and girl together.

"Ah! Mr. Terry, is that you?" said the housekeeper in her crisp tones; "and what brings you out so early in the morning?"

"Five o'clock is not so very early, is it?"

"'T is for some folks. You never used ter be so fond o' sp'ilin' yer paytent luthers."

Terry extended a foot and eyed the thin-soled shoe, small enough almost for a lady, with approval.

"Those are not 'paytent luthers,' my dear woman; they are the very best of French calf."

"What's the differ'nce?"

"As much difference as there is between old Peggy Scannell's black goat and one of those sleek cows yonder."

"Well, never mind," returned the house-keeper, composedly, "I knew there was ca'f somew'er's — only I never mistrusted 't was the boots!"

When Tabby showed her claws Terry always changed the subject.

"There goes a gray squirrel! a big fellow, too. Say, Tabby, do you ever make squirrel pie nowadays?"

"Hain't sence you was here afore. Nobody else 'll touch 'em."

"I 'll touch 'em then. Make me one, will you, Tabby?"

"Ef you 'll ketch the squirr'ls, an' skin 'em, and clean 'em, an' cut 'em up. I c'n put 'em in with a fork, but I 'd as lief have nothin' ter do with the butcherin'."

"I 'll ketch 'em," mimicked Terry again, drawing forth as he spoke a very shiny and elegant little revolver. Mrs. Bloom beat a precipitate retreat.

"Ain't ye *never* without that blunderbuss, night nor day?" she inquired incisively; "sh'd think 't was a stick o' candy, the way ye drop it inter yer pocket. Mark my words, Terry Jackson, it 'll bring ye ter repentance yet! There 's no good ever comes o' keepin' bad comp'ny; 'specially when the comp'ny 's liable ter bust up an' kill ye any minnit. 'Sides, ye don't need it here; there may be pirits an' candy balls down ter York, but we don't raise no sech crops round Ockley."

"Frogs will do for pirates, and I 'll act cannibal myself. Don't be scared, Tabby; I like waffles too well to shoot you."

"Might as well shoot a body as scare 'em

ter death," retorted Mrs. Bloom. " Come, clear out o' there now ! I 'm goin' ter sweep."

" And you want to make a clean sweep, don't you, Tabby? Well, I 'll forgive you, and bring you the ' squirr'ls ' too."

" Don't hurt yerself ter do either," quoth the housekeeper, with dry energy, as the young man moved off ; " both on 'em 's works o' sup'reragashin, as the parson says ! "

CHAPTER XII.

"Had he stayed to weigh and to scan,
He had been more or less than a man."

CHRISTINA ROSSETTI.

Cy eyed Terry with apprehension as the fishing party assembled on the lawn. Fortunately for their plans, however, all that appeared was a very handsome English rod and a fly-book of unusual perfection and elegance of appointment. Terry considered the use of bait quite too rustical even when after such small fry as perch or pickerel.

Robin did not go; she had given up excursions of late. She said it was because dog-days made frequent churning necessary, and the dairy needed her. But Mrs. Bloom shook her fat head a good deal over this statement; though all she said was: —

"Glad ter see ye so prewdent! Guess that two days' headache done ye good. I never knew dogs, nor 'cats-'n'-dogs' ter stop ye afore."

Something had stopped her now, however; she stood on the steps with her uncle as the wagon rolled off, and waved a blithe little handkerchief in response to the waving hats. Then she turned, and went in, with a song on her lips, to her morning's work of ordering and beautifying the house. She hurried it a little to-day, for Conrad had left her the latest chapters of his book, and she wanted to get away under the trees with them, the better to consider and criticise at her leisure. Mrs. Bloom, who was never to be prevented from " seein' threw a millstone when ther' was a hole in it," followed her mistress's quick movements with a watchful eye; and when Robin passed out through the kitchen, manuscript in hand, on her way to the orchard, said eye twinkled knowingly as she remarked, —

" C'nclewded ter let the cream saour, hain't ye?"

" No," replied Robin, innocently. " I churned this morning."

" H'm! why didn't ye let me help ye? Balled it yet?"

" No, it will ball better when it has been kept cold awhile."

" An' when some one's ter hum ter help!" amended the housekeeper under her breath, watching the girl's pretty figure passing slowly up between the trees. " 'T 's unfort'nit Terry 's took t' early risin' also. The proverb don't say nothin' 'baout the early bird's findin' *tew* worms. Wonder what she 'll do with 'em ! "

Meanwhile the fishing-party had reached its destination so far as horse and wagon were concerned. These were put up at the farm-house nearest the pond; and the gentlemen, having arranged with the farmer for the use of his boat, shouldered their accoutrements, and, preceded by Cy bearing the generous dinner - basket, filed down through the barn-yard and across the vegetable garden and pasture to the point of embarkation.

The boat was a square cut, clumsy, homemade affair, and the oars were roughly shaped from wood to which, in some places, the bark was yet clinging. Terry made a grimace as he took possession of that which he was to handle and felt its weight and general unwieldiness. Conrad had used them more recently; he took his place, quietly, and turned the boat about. Cy and the basket, as ballast, were placed amidships.

"Now then, Joe," said Terry, "just tell us " —

" My name ain't Joe," muttered Cy, casting uneasy glances toward the speaker.

" It ought to be then, if it is n't. Which of these numerous shores are we to steer for?"

" Mister Forkner," said Cy, ignoring all other human presence, " d' ye see that little kind 'er p'int that runs out there east o' the island, that one with a big pitch pine on the end?" Conrad looked in the direction indicated.

" Yes, Cy, I see. Shall we make for that?"

" That 's the best place fer perch. Ef ye want pick'rel ye must go over yonder in the shadder; there where all them weeds is."

" There does n't seem to be much ' shadder ' anywhere to-day," remarked Terry. " Ockley fish are the only ones I ever saw that were fools enough to bite in a hot sun like this." But he gave his ponderous oar a backward sweep that brought the boat's head — if a craft alike stubbed at both ends can be said to have a head — about, slowly, in the required direction. Ten minutes' rowing brought them to the point, and

Conrad, laying aside his oar, dropped the heavy stone which served for anchor quietly down into the oily black water.

In the shadow of the big pitch pine they sat and fished. Whether it was because, as Terry had said, they were Ockley fish and therefore fools; or whether, after the monotonous worm offered by the country lads for their temptation and destruction, they found Terry's delicate little flies too irresistible to be neglected, certain it is that, in spite of the bright sunshine and a provoking little breeze which sprang up and ruffled the surface of the pond, the fish bit well, and every few moments one or the other line came flying through the air, each with its little red-finned struggler securely hooked. Presently, however, as the breeze increased and the flies became an old story, the intervals between luck grew longer, till Terry's stock of patience. never too great, gave out, and he began to reel up in disgust.

"This is working rather hard for pleasure, don't you think so, Con? Here we have been at it for two mortal hours, and only two dozen miserable little things to show for it! Cy, these are not perch at all; they 're nothing but shiners."

" Ef ye want ter try fer pick'rel, Mister Forkner, mebbe they 'd bite better. The island 'd be between us an' the wind, an' they 're dreadful greedy fellers, anyhow."

Conrad, whose mind, to tell the truth, was anywhere but on what he was doing, acquiesced silently, and drew in his line also. Perch or pickerel, it mattered little to him; his thoughts were busy with things that had to do with far more vital issues. Ever since the day when Terry's coming had so inopportunely cut short what he had meant to tell Robin, he had sought in vain for a chance to begin again. Terry was ubiquitous, and Robin was, largely, an absentee. She left the two young men, for the most part, to each other; except as they drove or walked all together, or gathered for music in the evening, and in that realm Terry was king.

There were no *tête-à-têtes* for anybody. To be sure Terry had only been there a week, but it seemed like an age after the easy, hourly companionship that had gone before. Conrad's days were fast becoming numbered, too; only two weeks to the first of September, and he must not disappoint the Thachers. All this was in his thoughts as he pulled his oar in time with Terry's and changed his small hook for a larger one. Declining the combination of peacock's feathers which Terry offered, with the assurance that it was "a killer," he baited with a bit of perch, and casting his line well over in the "shadder" sat waiting, with eyes fixed on the gray rocks and coarse, thin grass of the island, strewn with pine needles from the gaunt trees which shadowed them.

"I say, Con, if you don't mean to land that fellow I wish you'd give some one else a chance!" exclaimed Terry, under his breath, when they had fished, in silence, for half an hour at least. "He'll have your bait in another minute."

Conrad started from his reverie and the pickerel scurried off, taking the bit of perch with him.

"There, I'm done!" cried Terry, impatiently; "that is the only one that has showed his snout at all; and now he's gone off with a week's provisions. These confounded fish don't know a high-toned fly when they see it; a worm on a bent pin is about the style of thing that obtains here."

"Mebbe ye'll feel better when ye've hed yer dinner," suggested Cy. "There's a real

good place ter camp down in over under
them big oak-trees, ef ye don't mind rowin'
a little ter git there."

The oak-trees were across the pond again.
Another pull in the hot sun. But the spot
repaid them when they reached it, for the
oaks cast a dense, cool shade, and among the
rocks was a spring. They ate the bountiful
lunch which Mrs. Bloom's forethought had
provided; and then Conrad strolled off,
among the trees, leaving Terry and Cy
stretched out in lazy comfort, beside the
remnants of the feast.

He sat himself down, after a while, on the
trunk of a fallen tree; and by dint of some
pretty hard thinking came to a determination. This uncertainty and procrastination
were not to be endured. He verily believed
his brain would give way if he thought it all
over much longer. He would not spend another night like the past three or four; it
should be either better or worse, come what
would. He would have an hour with Robin
alone, and say his say, even if he had to
speak out plainly to Terry and tell him that
he was *de trop*. That Terry's burr-like pro-
clivities might be based upon a like objection to himself had never dawned upon his
mind.

Having reached a decision he felt better. The breeze blew freshly toward him, over the lake, and for the first time that day he yielded to its soothing touch and, half lying on the grass, half leaning against the tree-trunk, gave himself up to repose. He drew a book from his coat-pocket; a quaint little book, "The Family of Sir Thomas More," which Robin had lent him from her own special book-shelves; and beginning to read, somewhat carelessly, was soon taken possession of by the simple beauty of the chronicle, and became lost to all around him. Presently Terry, tired of Cy and the broken fragments, came to look him up. Terry was no book-worm; he perched himself on the old tree, and, thinking in his turn pretty deeply, for him, apparently amused himself by throwing acorns into the pond. A half hour went by.

"Con!" said Terry.

No answer. Conrad was deep in his book.

"I say — Con!" and he shied an acorn at the small volume with accurate aim.

Conrad quietly brushed it off, and went on reading.

"By Jove, I'll fetch him!" muttered Terry to himself, and rapidly accumulating a handful of full and empty cups he dashed them, *en masse*, upon the printed page which was proving so inconveniently absorbing.

"Hulloa, Terry! what's the matter now?" inquired his friend, looking up in surprise at this sudden onslaught.

"You're a fine sociable chap, are n't you?" said Terry, mockingly. "I've hardly been able to get a word with you since I've been here. After all these weeks of stewing in silence, down yonder, I feel like saying something semi-occasionally. You could n't stop reading, for five minutes or so, and talk to anybody, could you?"

"Yes, I could," said Conrad, dumping the *débris* and closing his book, "fire away, old fellow!" and he threw himself back on the grass, after the approved masculine fashion, with his locked hands supporting the back of his head, and his straw hat tipped over his face.

Thus encouraged Terry sat silent for the first three of his stipulated five minutes. Conrad munched a grass-stalk and watched him, amusedly, from under the hat-brim.

"Have n't swallowed your tongue, have you?" he inquired, anxiously, at length.

Terry certainly swallowed something pretty hard before he answered, but then his words came out with a sudden impulse which proved his powers of articulation unimpaired.

" What do you think of Robin ? "

The question was totally unexpected. It shot like an arrow of light into Conrad's brain, and for one terrible instant every nerve in his body seemed to contract with the shock of what the words, or the tone in which they were spoken, revealed to him. He had not made character study his business for so long to remain stupidly blind now to what lay hidden under such a question from such a source. He knew Terry through and through. He could always read his meaning, and had read it often, in lighter words than these, — words which others let pass as merely " Jackson's nonsense." He read it now. He knew, from that moment, what, wrapped in his own hopes and dreams, he had never surmised before. Terry was in love with Robin. There was no reason why he should not be, if he wanted to ; they were only cousins by marriage after all. It was no recent tumble either; it must have been going on for years. Would she — did she already — had she indeed for years also returned the feeling ? Was this the explana-

tion of all her frank, beautiful comradeship?
Was the fact of his being Terry's best friend
the reason, the only reason, of her own readily yielded friendliness? Was the brightest
summer of his life to end in darkness such
as this? He could have groaned aloud in
agony of spirit, but he did not. People
don't, commonly, when other people are by.
He only compressed years of suffering into a
two-minutes' draught and drank it down in
silence, under his hat, while Terry, glancing
impatiently at the friendly head-gear, detected no slightest ruffling of its sunburned serenity.

"Well," he broke out, suddenly, "are n't
you going to say anything?"

The strong white teeth closed on the grass-
stalk and gave it a fearful bite.

"What do you want me to say?"

"Say? why, say what you think! She's
beautiful is n't she — for one thing?"

"Very." How the word hurt him!

"Is n't she one girl in a thousand?"

Conrad was silent. He could not answer
such a question as that. What had thousands or ten thousands to do with her, the
one woman in all God's universe to him?

"What is it that makes her so? Come,

old fellow, you pretend to a vast amount of insight; you've a mighty sharp nose for the reasons of things, — what's the reason of this?"

"I cannot tell."

"Then I am smarter than you, for once, for I can. She's round!"

"Round?" repeated Conrad mechanically.

"Yes, round; symmetrical, if you like it better.   There are no rough spots and no sharp edges.   Her face and figure and brain are all proportioned to each other. Her eyes are as beautiful as her voice, and her voice is as well modulated as her motions. She is as good as she is beautiful, and as graceful as she is good.   When she is sober you feel as if a smile would spoil her, and when she laughs you wonder why you ever wanted her to do anything else.   She is the most — but hang it all! why am I yarning all this off to you. I wonder? and there you lie soaking it all in as still as a sponge!"

"Why not, since of course it is all true?"

How true it was he knew better than Terry could possibly tell him. Was not his heart indorsing every word with a fresh throb of pain?

"Oh, well, you can laugh, I suppose. It's

no such laughing matter to me. But then, you 're not in love with her."

The straw hat lay motionless.

" It 's a wonder, too, mind you," pursued Terry, musingly. " I 've been beastly afraid of it, you know."

" Have you ? "

Something curious in the tone of these two words made Terry look round. But as nothing met his eyes save the down-tipped hat, with a long stem of timothy protruding from beneath it, he ascribed the peculiar accent to semi-suffocation and sailed on.

" You see, Con, you 've a way with you, when you like."

" Have I ? "

" Yes, you have!" reiterated Terry, beginning to wax impatient of these brief, interrogatory answers. " And it 's a mighty winning way, too."

" Is it ? "

" Confound it all ! " cried the badgered youth, leaping to his feet and with one well-directed blow knocking the other's slight screen into a barberry bush; " drop your laconics, old man ! What do you want to choke yourself to death with your own hat for ? "

Conrad laughed and drew himself lazily

up into the shade ; but there was a contrac-
tion about his eyes and forehead as of pain.
Perhaps the sudden sunshine dazzled him.

" What 's the matter with you, Con ? got a
headache ? "

" No — yes — nothing ! Get to the point,
man, for Heaven's sake, if there is a point,
and let 's get away out of this fearful heat ! "

" There is n't any point, just at present,
but I mean there shall be before I go back to
the city. I promised Uncle Ike not to say
a word for two years, but the two years are
more than up now, and I 've got a good many
words to say."

" You promised your uncle ? " said Conrad,
speaking slowly and with difficulty. " Then
the matter is already understood in the family."

" Of course. Robin and I grew up together, you know. It has always been straight
sailing till old Crabbe went and got the gollywobbles. You must confess," he hurried
on, laughing a trifle consciously, " that it has
been pretty rough on me to stay behind and
know there was another fellow — and a better one — up here where I wanted to be.
But I see that 's all right now. Robin is not
the girl to desert old friends for new ones.

There's no harm done,— and you'll wish me joy old fellow, won't you?"

He held out his hand to his friend, sure of his sympathy, and his friend did not fail him. But as Conrad yielded to the other's hearty pressure the first two lines of Launcelot Owen's epitaph burned themselves, like fire, into his memory. Was this why he had felt that strange thrill of spiritual kinship?

> "God gave me a hard daye's worke
> But I did not shirke."

"And I will not shirk!" he said proudly to himself as he strode slowly back, after Terry, to their place of landing. "The 'rest' will come at last."

It did not begin to come as yet, though. The amount of slow torture which human nature can endure, and yet stand on its feet and give no sign, is fearful to realize. Conrad walked on mechanically, like one in a terrible, dumb dream. His sight was introverted, reading the sharp, transfixing sentence that the last half hour had written, in black characters, across the one bright chapter of his life. Even had there been hope for him, he must, in common honor, have stood aside for Terry's prior claim ; and there was no hope. " Robin is not the girl to desert old friends for new ones!" How well he knew the truth of Terry's words.

So absorbed was he in his own trouble that he never saw Cy sitting, unconscious of their approach, under one of the generous old trees. Terry saw, however, and noticed that the fat boy was intent upon something. Following the direction of his gaze he discovered a large gray squirrel seated on the lowest limb of another tree near by and watching, in his turn, the boy. It reminded him of something which he had been near forgetting: the material for Mrs. Bloom's pie. He raised his hand softly, and thrust it into his left breast pocket.

From beneath the oak where Cy lay, motionless, came a low, chittering sound. The squirrel ran down the branch to its very end, and stopped, his black eyes shining, his full, feathery brush giving little spasmodic jerks. The low call came again. Could there be another squirrel down there among the bushes? The black eyes and bushy tail came nearer, their gray owner approaching warily over the soft grass. Within ten feet of Cy's resting-place he came to a halt, raised himself upon his little haunches and sniffed the air questioningly. Something flashed in the sunlight, as Terry raised his hand with steady aim. Conrad, catching sight of it all too late, made a hasty rush forward, and shouted. Cy turned his head, and saw the detested revolver gleaming in Terry's grasp. The blind rage that was one of the few evidences of his mental deficiency took possession of him; and never stopping to see that the squirrel had fled at the first alarm, he rushed frantically forward, and wrenched the weapon from its owner's hand.

It was at full cock. There came a blaze, a report, and poor Cy lay in a heap on the ground with a 22-calibre ball in his side.

CHAPTER XIII.

OWEN MEREDITH.

UP in the hill orchard some one was singing like a bobolink. The clear, liquid notes came floating down beneath overarching, fruit-laden boughs and floated in at the library windows where the parson sat and smiled to hear them.

"Happy and free-hearted as ever, my Robin-red-breast!" he thought to himself. "Terry may have to wait a bit after all. She does not tire of the old home or the old man yet. Just as well, just as well! the boy is a good boy, but he is young and, sometimes, he seems a little selfish, a little selfish like his father. If only he were more like — but there! 'comparisons are odious,' and girls will choose for themselves."

The breeze blew over the lawn again and brought another snatch of the old song. Bending forward, the parson could see the girl, in her white dress, moving among the gnarled old trunks of the apple-trees. She held in her hand the manuscript she had been reading, but her eyes were searching the green wilderness overhead and her lips were overflowing with melody.

> " In a fair wood like this, where the beeches are growing,
>   Brave Robin Hood hunted in days of old:
>   Down his broad shoulders his brown locks fell flowing;
>   His cap was of green, with a tassel of gold."

A farm horse, ridden bareback by a small, barefooted, sunburned boy, came clumsily cantering down the road. Robin's eyes followed the moving object, half unconsciously ; while the sweet voice sang on : —

> " His eye was as blue as the sky in midsummer;
>   Ruddy his cheek as the oak-leaves in June;
>   Hardy his voice as he hailed the new-comer,
>   Tender to maidens in changeable tune."

The horse stopped at the gate, and the boy slid off and tied the end of the leather halter, which served as bridle, to the fence. For one moment a thrill of apprehension, as of some bad tidings, swept over the girl ; but the messenger had gone round to the kitchen door ; some errand to Mrs. Bloom, probably. She passed up, through the orchard, to the boundary wall and went on

with her ballad, looking off, over the river,
to the fair, far-away hills.

> " His step had a strength, and his smile had a sweetness;
>   His spirit was wrought of the sun and the breeze;
>   He moved as a man framed in Nature's completeness,
>   And grew unabashed with the growth of the trees."

The barefooted boy had come out again
and Mrs. Bloom followed him. The former
sprawled himself onto his beast's back and
cantered off as he had come; the latter
came up, over the short orchard grass, to
her mistress; moving slowly, as if weighted
with a heavy message.

> " I think, as I lie in the shade of the beeches,
>   How lived and how loved this old hero of song;
>   I wish we could follow the lesson he teaches,
>   And dwell, as he dwelt, these wild thickets among;
>   At least for a while, till we caught up the meaning
>   The beeches breathe out in the wealth of their growth;
>   Width in their nobleness, love in their leaning " —

" Miss Robin, my dear ! "

Robin turned her head; her eyes, with a
dreamy, preoccupied look in them, rested on
the housekeeper's face. But no sooner did
she catch its expression than she started
forward, the dreamy look all gone.

" What is it? what has happened ? " the
nameless dread came back and took possession of her.

" There, there, my dear ! don't you take

on now, don't! 'T ain't as ef 't was Master
Terry, though I don't know but it's wicked
of me ter say so when the poor feller may
be a-dyin'."

"Who is it? what is it?" cried the girl,
in a desperate whisper. "Tell me! quick!"
and she fairly shook the portly woman in
her eager terror.

"Why," began Mrs. Bloom, slowly, striving to be composed and only succeeding
in being exasperating, "Master Terry was
shootin' somethin' an' — the other chap
tried ter stop him, an' — ter tell the trewth
I dunno exactly *haow* 't was, but the pistil
went off, anyways, as I've alwers expected
't would, some day, an' hit him."

"Hit *who?*" almost shrieked Robin, patience and grammar alike deserting her in
the same sharp breath. "Not — not" —

She could not have spoken his name just
then to save her life. She did not need to;
Mrs. Bloom had not been seeing through
millstones all summer for nothing.

"Not Mister Forkner? Land alive, *no*,
child! *Cy*, Cy's the one that's hurt.
Terry 'll hev ter git up earlier 'n he done
this mornin' ter blow Mister Forkner's
brains out! Ye might ha' knowed that."

Her mistress took no notice of her. Shock and counter-shock had followed one another so quickly that they came near being too much for her. Another kind of girl would have fainted; Robin only clutched the sharp stones of the wall till they cut her hands, and turned from white to red, and from red to white again with startling rapidity. The housekeeper's sharp eyes saw and understood it all; but she was a shrewd woman, and stood quiet till the tense, clinging fingers had loosened their grasp and lay helpless. Then she said : —

"They 're up ter 'Biram Woods's, an' they want ye ter send up the spring-wagon, with some pillers an' things, ter fetch him hum in. Leastways they *said* the parson, but I knew *he* would n't know nothin' what ter do."

Robin turned, without a word, and flew down the orchard and into the house as if she had had wings.

"First down an' then up, that 's her all over!" groaned Mrs. Bloom, as she followed more heedfully. "*She* 'll never endure ter hev three on 'em as I hev."

In which declaration Robin would most assuredly have upheld her.

The parson, sitting peacefully by his window, was suddenly startled by beholding first a mattress, and then a shower of pillows, come flying down, from the clouds apparently, to the grass-plot before him. Then Mrs. Bloom was seen hurrying to the barn, with her apron over her head, and in another minute Robin came into the room, with her hat on and traces of recent tears about her eyes.

"Uncle Ike," she said, "we are wanted up at Abiram Woods's. Terry has contrived to let his revolver go off hind-side-before, somehow, and Cy is hurt."

"You don't say so!" exclaimed the parson, springing to his feet and seizing the hat that always lay handy. "That *is* bad news. But why do you assume that it is Terry's fault, my dear?"

"I know it must be his fault. Cy never meddles with things that do not concern him. But here is the wagon; we won't stop to talk about it now. Put in all those things, Abijah, and Mrs. B. just hand me that big umbrella. Now, Uncle Ike, we must drive fast!"

It was a silent drive. The parson was trying to account satisfactorily to himself for the accident, and wondering how revolvers should have been in requisition on a fishing excursion : while in Robin's mind gladness for Conrad's immunity and sorrow for Cy's misfortune were waging tumultuous warfare.

As they drove up to the door of the farmhouse Terry, rather pale but trying hard to look unconcerned, appeared from within.

" Well, Robin, your *protégée* has been getting himself into hot water ! Nothing very alarming, though, the doctor thinks."

Robin vouchsafed him not even a glance, but, putting one foot on the wheel, sprang past him and entered the stuffy little room off the kitchen, where Cy lay. Mrs. Woods was sitting by the bedside armed with a palm-leaf fan, which she waved vigorously to and fro to drive away the flies ; talking, the while to Conrad, who stood by the window. He came forward to meet Robin, when she entered, and spoke reassuringly of Cy as Terry had done ; but his face looked worn and grave, and he presently passed out upon the stoop to see that the farmer and his man were in readiness to help lift.

Robin wondered a little. His manner was not at all as usual, even allowing for the un-

usual circumstances ; but this was no time
for such considerations ; Cy was waiting, and
must be gotten home at once. She went
back to the wagon and busied herself with
mattress and pillows till all was arranged to
her liking. Then the four men lifted the
wounded boy, finding their united strength
none too much for the skillful accomplishment of the task, and laid him gently down
upon the soft bed provided for him. Robin
said nothing to him, for he seemed to shun
being spoken to, lying with closed eyes, for
the most part, and feigning sleep ; though
she knew well there could be no sleep for
him in his present condition, jolting along
over roads whose frequent roughnesses even
the spring-wagon and well-arranged cushions
were powerless to overcome. So she only
took care that the big umbrella should in-
cline always at just the right angle, and that
the well side should take the brunt of the
jouncing as the parson drove carefully on,
avoiding, as much as was possible, all stones
and cradle-holes in his way.

Terry and Conrad, in their own wagon,
had taken a shorter and rougher cut to the
village to prepare Janet and the cottage
for Cy's reception. Neither required much

preparation ; the house was always ready, to the extent of its resources, for anything, and its owner had been brought face to face with trouble too often, in her checkered life, to fear it when it came. So, after hearing them out, quietly, she turned with only an added gravity in her face, a slight compression of the lips, and went on with her task of ironing Cy's Sunday shirt, which must not be left to mildew for want of care though the poor fellow was little likely to need it for some time to come. Meanwhile, the two gentlemen, with a neighbor or two to assist in the lifting, stood waiting at the steps till the parson drove up.

Cy opened his eyes and looked at his grandmother, then closed them again and lay passive while the men transferred him from wagon to bed. When he was fairly established and made comfortable his grandmother bent over and kissed him, and again he opened his eyes and looked at her. That was all. The one a woman, refined above her station, the other a clumsy, half-witted boy, they yet had thus much in common beside their kinship : that they were at once too proud and too innately delicate to demonstrate, largely, either grief or affection while other eyes were looking on. Conrad lingered by the bedside as Robin and her uncle passed out into the kitchen with Janet. He bent over the boy and said, with feeling, —

"You are a brave fellow, Cy! I shall stay by to see you well out of this. If I had only kept my word a little better you would not have been lying here now."

The fat boy opened his eyes once more and smiled up into his friend's face, — a smile of love and gratitude which came straight from his heart, and wore the beauty such looks ever do wear independently of any blemish of mere feature. The affection and trust, and a vague something undefined which seemed to be conveyed in that one look, were too much for the young man; he turned abruptly away and followed the others out. As he gained the foot of the steps the parson turned from handing Robin into the vehicle, and evidently expected him to follow. Terry and the other equipage had disappeared.

"Mr. Cary," said Conrad, pausing a little over his words as though he found them hard to say, "I think it will be better for me not to go back to Saints' Rest with you.

Janet needs some one with strong arms to help her, and Cy will let me do for him as he will not let a stranger. Besides, I feel in a measure accountable for his trouble, and must see him on the road to recovery before I leave."

"Leave! My dear boy, what are you talking about? September is two weeks off yet."

"I know," replied Conrad, and one quick ear at least caught the repressed pain in his voice; "but my plans have changed, unavoidably, since morning. Had it not been for this accident I should have returned to Boston to-morrow. I have had — news which calls me away from Ockley."

The parson was just the least bit deaf. He caught words readily enough, but the nice shadings of tone were wont to escape him. He took Conrad's answer at its letter, which was as well, perhaps.

"News? not bad news, I hope; not" — He paused, with the peculiar look of impending condolence on his face which people wear when they are not quite certain whether there will prove to be a use for it or not.

"Not sickness, nor death, no. But I must go, for all that," said Conrad, gravely.

Only I shall wait to see Cy better, first. I can be more useful to him here than two miles off ; so if you will kindly let Abijah bring my trunk to the hotel I shall be greatly obliged. I am more sorry than I can say to break away from your hospitality so suddenly ; but it is not really good-by yet, you know," he added, trying to smile.

"Good-by? I should think not! Let us hope you won't have to go, after all. Abijah shall bring your trunk down, if you wish, of course, but had n't you better reconsider that part of it? I shall be driving down daily, as usual, and Robin will be with Janet most of the time, if I know her."

"Thank you," said Conrad, quietly, " but my place seems to be here, just now. My holiday has been a rare one, thanks to you both, but it is over!" And he raised his hat, and stepped aside to let them pass.

Somehow, there was nothing to be said. The parson was surprised, and sorry, but could find no good reason for combating his guest's decision. As for Robin, she could not have spoken a word if she had wanted to ; her heart was too full. She hardly dared look up lest Conrad should see what an effect his words had produced.

Her uncle wondered, as they drove home, at the depth of her interest in Cy, as manifested by her unusually grave and subdued demeanor.

CHAPTER XIV.

ROBIN was sitting in the cool darkness, on the wide east stoop, alone. She had come here on purpose to be alone, and to think; leaving Terry and her uncle talking together at the front of the house. It was just five hours since they had parted from Conrad in the village street. It seemed five years. Only this morning all had been as usual; no cloud to mar the happy serenity of their daily life, except, indeed, the little, indefinable cloud, hardly as big as " a man's hand," of light restraint that Terry's presence had thrown over their former unreserved companionship. Yet that had only been for a week; it was but common courtesy to set aside their old ways a little out of deference to a new-comer. Conrad was still free to propose walks or drives, if he liked. And she had been so sure he

would like; so sure that their interfered-
with afternoon of last week would be made
good ere the end of this.   And lo, a thun-
derbolt from a blue sky!

Robin buried her head in her hands and
thought — and thought. " Since morning ; "
those were his words. But he had read all his
letters before leaving the house, she knew,
and no communication could have reached
him out on Porter's Pond with Cy and Terry.
With Terry! Ah, the light flashed upon her
now ! The hands unclasped, the head was
thrown back, proudly, in the darkness. She
was not blind nor deaf ; she had known for a
good while past what was simmering in her
cousin's mind. She had thrown in an occasional dash of cold water, too, as opportunity
offered; but he was only a boy, after all ;
he was wont to have sudden freaks in other
matters and get over them again ; somehow
she had never attached much weight to this.
It was only a phase. A little tonic snub,
once in a while, kept him pretty straight,
and he would grow wiser in time. But
now, if he had boiled over — to Conrad !
She sprang to her feet and clenched her
pretty hands into little redoubtable fists as
she thought of it. Ridiculous! how could

Conrad credit such a thing for a moment?
Was this his notion of friendship, to let
the silly talk of a boy come between them
now, when he ought to know her so well?
And then the hands relaxed, and a warm
glow shot from heart to face as she remembered how he had looked and spoken. She
smiled to herself, in the darkness, well
pleased to think what her hold upon his life
must be since even a false impression could
give him such pain in passing. For it would
pass, of course it would. Had he not given
her his promise that no third person should
ever interfere between them? He would
never leave Ockley without giving her at
least a chance to explain. And she *would*
explain; there should be no heroic false
pride about her. What a mercy that he
had been kept from starting off at a tan-
gent! She should have opportunity still to
prove to him how utterly foundationless
Terry's castles were. Then she remembered
what had kept him, and her indignation with
Terry broke forth afresh. Was it not
enough, for one day's work, to have made
two people miserable, but he must pretty
nearly kill a third? Poor Cy! to whom it
seemed as if sufficient had been denied al-

ready, shut up all through this sunny summer-time he so loved and reveled in, just because a thoughtless boy had valued his own momentary gratification above a poor, half-witted fellow's simple pleasure. Cy, a fool! there was great question in her mind as to which was the greater fool of the two! The idea of any human being, who pretended to the possession of brain, shooting at a squirrel with a ball like that! One would think the game had been a buffalo!

She laughed out to herself at the thought and then caught herself up in a hurry. What if Terry should hear? Too late! he had heard; and the next moment the rustling of the grass warned her that he was coming. Meet him again that night she would not! She sprang out into the darkness and fled, noiselessly and fleetly, round the opposite corner of the house. Before he could discover her flight and follow she was safe in her own room with the door bolted. Once there, strangely enough, all her newly built up hopes dissipated themselves into thin air. The whole burden of pain and misery that the day had brought to herself and others rushed over her in a flood which she felt powerless to stem. She threw herself into

the big, chintz-covered chair by the window
and cried as she had never cried in all her
life before. Yet, sooth to say, her tears,
after all, were more for her friend's pain
than her own.

Meantime this friend, at the little village
hotel, was having his thoughts too, and un-
locking his trunk in search of needed articles for Cy. The first thing that met his
eyes, lying where he had himself put it that
morning to keep it out of harm's — Mrs.
Bloom's — way, was the unfinished painting
of Janet's cottage. He smiled, half bitterly,
as he saw it and remembered the afternoon
when it had been begun. How different
had been the evening of that day from this!
The scarlet columbine, for which he had
plunged and scrambled at the risk of his
neck through the darkness by the river, was
lying safe, in its withered brightness, in his
little pocket dictionary, from whose pages
they had once stood to read together the
definition of a certain word. What had become of the friendship they had plighted
then? Had it, too, withered and faded like
the flower? Nay, he knew but too well that,
on his side at least, it had blossomed into
such glorious sweetness as he had never

dreamed of in all his life before. Only, "it takes two to make a bargain." Robin had done all she bargained to do; there had been no failure on her side; the trouble lay in the fact that he had done vastly more on his part than the contract called for, and they had need to make their bargain all over again or — cancel it forever. The waves of trouble were dashing over him now as they were dashing over Robin, at her chamber window, only two short miles away. But neither could read the other's thoughts, and the soft, warm wind, blowing straight from him to her, told no tales. Memory after memory came surging back upon his heart as he stood there, motionless, the picture in his hand. The thought of that evening on the Ridge, when they had stood together in the moonlight and Robin had sung for him, came back, with a new, terrible sting in its sweetness, and mastered him. Once more the full, rich tones were sounding all about him. How full of promise had seemed the words she sung.

> "Oh, rest in the Lord; wait patiently for Him,
> And He shall give thee thy heart's desire."

His heart's desire! he had thought then that he knew what that was. And those beautiful words of the Invocation had been like a prayer for blessing upon them both. Again the melody was beating round him in a flood; the sweet breath of the wild-grape blossoms floated near, and Robin's face looked up at him in the moonlight. He started as a great brown beetle, attracted by the reeking warmth and light of his kerosene lamp, came booming in at the open window. There was no moon to-night, and out of the darkness below came up the faint squeak of the hostler's fiddle.

"Pshaw, I am a fool!" he exclaimed, bitterly; and blowing out the light, went fumbling down the steep, narrow staircase to the street.

Janet saw nothing to wish otherwise in either his looks or attentions that night, as he shared the watch by Cy's bedside and ministered to his wants as tenderly as a brother could have done. But the fat boy, taught by some half-smothered instinct in his own heart, and his great love for his friend, looked up into Conrad's face with wistful eyes that read the bravely hidden pain and guessed its cause.

CHAPTER XV.

"For life was bitter through those words repressed."
JEAN INGELOW.

"Ben," said Miss Constance, as she handed her brother his second cup of coffee, "the boy is in trouble."

"H'm!" returned the lawyer, glancing down the second page of the letter that lay beside his plate; "I should say it was the fat friend who was in trouble. Con's whole-footed yet, as far as I see."

"I see farther than you do, Ben."

"The deuce you do! may be you see double, old lady."

"He is in trouble;" repeated Miss Constance, slowly, holding out her hand for the letter; "I see it in every word."

"You see a heap of it, take it altogether, then."

"His visit is not ending as he hoped, and I expected, it would end," pursued the lady, paying no heed to the remarks of her skeptical brother.

" And how the — how *did* you expect it
to end ? " asked Mr. Thacher, awaiting her
reply with his coffee-cup half way to his
lips.

" I expected it would end in an engage-
ment."

The lawyer stared ; then he took a hasty
gulp of the coffee, which proved to be pretty
hot, and set his cup down upon its saucer
with a sharp click.

" Thank the Lord," he exclaimed, slowly,
" I 'm not a woman ! "

" The Lord knew what He was about when
He made you, my dear, as He always does,"
returned his sister calmly.

" It 's hard enough," went on Mr. Thacher,
" to face trouble when it comes ; but this tal-
ent for sighting the tail of a tragedy ten
miles off, and never winking again for fear
you should lose sight of it before it gets here,
is something exclusively feminine, which, I
feel moved to remark, I 'm devoutly thankful men don't, as a rule, possess ! "

" I told you long ago that Conrad was in
love with this girl, which I must confess is
hardly to be wondered at."

" And was n't that bad enough for a young
fellow with something under two thousand a

year to live on, but you must needs get him as good as engaged, and then smash up the whole thing? How do you know the boy is in trouble?"

Miss Constance silently handed back the letter.

"I've read it once. There's nothing written in sympathetic ink, I suppose!"

"Suppose you read it again, with sympathetic eyes, Ben."

Ben took the sheet once more and did as he was bid. When he got through he cleared his throat and blew his nose.

"Well?" said his sister.

"Well!" repeated the lawyer, unwillingly; "of course I see what you mean, now that you've put it into my head; but I defy any third person to see it. The boy's been sitting up nights, and worrying over that sick chap. Great good his holiday will do him at this rate! It's time he came back to us. Write to him, to-day, Connie, and tell him so. He'll be better off painting old Victory than dancing after a girl that's too big a fool to appreciate him."

Miss Constance sighed. "The girl is no fool, Ben; there has been some misunderstanding, I am sure. How I wish I could set it right!"

" What 's the use of wanting to set things right before you know what set them wrong? You 're a regular woman, Connie! May be Miss What 's-her-name wants somebody with more money and less brain."

" Ah, Ben! if you had only done as I wanted you to, and had told Conrad " —

" Fiddle-de-dee, child! would you have me throw out a bait to the fortune - hunters? No, no; the boy has better gold in his head and heart than we can ever put into his pocket. Time enough to pile on the spurious when some level-headed girl has found the true. Don't worry, Connie," he added, kindly; " I 'm as anxious to see the boy happily settled as you are, only I want him to find his wife while he 's poor. He 'll be a dar— he 'll be a deal more likely to find the right one. We can pitch in and make matrimony easy afterwards."

Miss Constance nodded approvingly, but the nod was followed up closely by another sigh. Evidently, being a " regular woman," she could not so easily get over the feminine yearning to " set it right."

" Get him here, get him here! " reiterated her brother, coming round for a good-by kiss before leaving the house. " You 'll fathom it, and set it right, too, if anybody can, but you must get him here first."

So when she had watched the roans off, down the avenue, Miss Constance seated herself at her secretary, and wrote as follows : —

MY DEAR BOY, — Ben and I are very sorry that your pleasant summer is having so sad an ending. Perhaps, however, matters will result more happily than you fear. Do not be too ready to renounce all hope. There may be some feature of the case which you do not as yet fully understand. Trust you have a good doctor. Of course, under the circumstances, we would not even *wish* to hurry you from Ockley until all is once more as it should be ; but September is close at hand, and your old room is always ready and waiting. We will hope for good news soon, and a blithe home-coming : but, merry or sad, remember that this *is* home and that a warm welcome awaits you.

Always your loving friend,
CONSTANCE M. THACHER.

"There!" said Miss Constance, laying down her pen with a deep breath of relief.

"I mean two things, and he will read two meanings, but I flatter myself he won't suspect they were put there on purpose!"

Could the good lady have been a "fly on the wall" when her doubly-worded note was received and read, she would have experienced a sinking of heart in both directions toward which its sentences were aimed.

Conrad was sitting at Cy's bedside while Janet snatched the brief sleep rendered indispensable by the night-watches which had been going on for more than two weeks now, and which she resolutely insisted upon sharing. They did not allow her to do much through the day, however. Either Robin or Conrad was always on hand, and sometimes, but this rarely, they were both there at once. At such times their outward relations appeared to others unchanged; but inwardly each felt the alteration, and each interpreted it in a different way.

Terry had walked down once since the accident, but his visit excited Cy beyond what was desirable, and he never came again.

Terry was rather put out by what he considered the "unnecessary fuss" made over the sick boy. "If Faulkner saw fit to make a fool of himself over a thing like that, let him! he, Terry, saw no adequate reason for such supreme devotion. The fellow brought it upon himself, and it did n't amount to anything anyhow. At this rate even old Crabbe would have proved more lively than anything he was likely to get in Ockley." So Robin went and came alone (went and stayed usually, now, for Cy grew no better, but rather lost ground, from day to day, as the unwonted confinement wore his strength away ; and Dr. Farnham had begun to look thoughtful and say little). and the breach between her and Conrad widened and widened. How often she had thought, with contempt, of the book - heroines who allowed small misunderstandings to swell, and lengthen to hundreds of pages of misery, when one bravely spoken word would have set all straight again — and spoiled the story! How firmly resolved she had been that no such silly weakness should ever cast a shadow over her own life-pages! yet here she was, after all, in the clutches of a like trouble, against which she was powerless. It makes such a difference whether one is an actor in the play or merely a looker-on! Could she rush up to Conrad Faulkner and say, " You

think I am in love with Terry, but I am
not?" How could she be sure that he did
think so? His bearing toward her was,
to all outward seeming, the same as ever;
she alone could feel that the friendship had
stopped growing. Besides, what time was
this for dwelling upon her own affairs when
they were all so worried over Cy? If anything beyond the sick-bed still troubled Conrad he never showed it now. His every
thought and care were for the patient, apparently. Perhaps he had ceased to care.
(She did not realize how successful her own
efforts for concealment were daily proving.)
If only he would say something, do something, ask some question which should give
her the opportunity she wanted! But no,
though he was kind and polite as ever, she
felt that he held himself aloof; and when,
this afternoon, he laid down his letter as
she appeared in the doorway, and treading
noiselessly with slippered feet, crossed the
floor to give her a chair and relieve her of
the basket which she carried, she felt the
walls of misunderstanding close in upon her
so unbearably that she well-nigh resolved to
dash them down with one desperate effort,
as Samson did the pillars of the house, even

though, like him, she should be overwhelmed, with all her future, in the ruins.

But Conrad gave her no opportunity. He came back presently from the well, whither he had gone for fresh water, and, setting the pitcher down on the table by the bed, beckoned her to the door.

"I see the doctor's chaise at his gate," he said as she joined him, "and think I will just step over and ask him to call before he starts off again. Cy seems to me not to be getting on as he should. He has a good deal of fever this afternoon, and at times is not quite clear-headed."

Robin tried to speak, but her heart was too full and the words choked her. He saw her trouble, but ascribed it all to anxiety for Cy.

"You must not worry," he said kindly; "perhaps it is only a notion of mine; but I think it will be as well to have Dr. Farnham's opinion; he has not been in since morning."

She bent her head, without speaking, and went back into the room. Conrad hurried away. Cy was awake when he returned with the doctor, but his eyes looked heavy and blood-shotten, and there was a deep crimson flush in his cheeks. A skillful physician's face might as well be a blank wall for all the expression that is allowed to come into it when examining a patient. Dr. Farnham was a skillful physician; and yet, though he went about his business with cool carefulness, gave his directions quietly as usual, and had a gay word for her at parting, Robin was sure he felt more anxiety about Cy than he admitted. She had seen that inscrutable face of his beside a good many sick-beds, and had learned to penetrate its professional mask beyond the ability of most people.

Janet had wakened from her nap and come in while he was there; and to her he had said, as if it were quite a matter of course : —

"You had better consent to have more help nights for a while, Mrs. Burns; why not get Mrs. Lake in to spell these folks a bit? Cy will probably be more or less restless, and you and I can't step as briskly as we once could. Mr. Faulkner here is used up. I have put him under strict orders to sleep." And with that, he walked off to his chaise, that waited for him in the street below, got in, and drove away.

Robin stood looking after the familiar vehicle, with its bob-tailed horse, till it turned a corner out of sight; and then continued to gaze at the spot where it had been, until roused by what Conrad was saying about getting Mrs. Lake to come in, as the doctor had advised. Janet was evidently rather averse to the arrangement.

"I shall stay with Janet to-night, Mr. Faulkner," said the girl, coming forward and laying her hand on her old nurse's arm; "she would rather have me than any one else, and I have done no night-work so far, while you have been getting tired out. It is my turn now. I told them at home that I should not be back till morning."

She stepped to the west window and threw open the blinds, which had been closed all day. The cool, sweet air wandered in refreshingly, and through the green foliage without shone glimpses of a golden and rose-colored sunset. Cy turned his tired eyes toward the distant brightness, and stopped for a moment his restless movements. Across the street, from the hotel, came the sound of the big bell accompanied by a clatter of dishes and the smell of hot bread. Conrad, seeing that he was

no longer needed, went over presently to his
tea and left the two women sitting in the
gathering twilight together.

Cy tossed and turned all night long, and
Janet was thankful enough for Robin's help
and company. The sick boy, who had always in health been so ready to come and
go at her bidding, now appeared to find her
presence more soothing, and her soft touch
more grateful, than any other. As the fever
increased, and rendered his poor brain more
misty than ever, he failed to recognize his
grandmother when she came to his side
with water or medicine, and would call for
" Miss Robin " to come and send her away.

Over and over he rehearsed the scene in
the woods at Porter's Pond; showing such
a nervous dread of Terry and his revolver
that Robin almost began to hate her cousin
for working such suffering and terror in the
poor fellow's life and mind. Towards morning he fell, at last, into an uneasy doze.
Janet had lain down on the wooden settle,
for a few minutes' rest, and was also asleep.
Robin moved quietly to the window, where
the early light was beginning to come in,
and drew the blinds, left open for freer air,
softly to. As she did so she caught sight

of Conrad passing from the hotel piazza to
the stables. Some minutes later she heard
the swish of wet grass, and his step coming
up to the door. She opened it.

"Miss Cary," he said, lowering his voice
(he never called her "Miss Robin" now),
"I am rested now and you are tired. One
of the hostlers will be over directly to drive
you up home. You will feel the need of a
hot breakfast and sound sleep such as can
only be had there. I shall stay with Cy for
the present."

She did not argue the matter with him as
she would have done a week before.

She put on her hat and shawl in silence,
and let him put her into the buggy, when it
came, also in silence. But she would not
drive off so; he had himself put a stop to the
old, happy friendliness which he had himself
been first to institute; but at least there
should be no noticeable change on her part.
She held out her hand, as he stood by the
step, and he took it for a moment in his.
Their eyes met in a brief look, and then the
horse started off, and he was left alone, in
the village street, with the touch of her hand
yet warm in his, and the memory of her half
questioning, half reproachful look haunting
him in spite of himself.

What did it mean? Was she hurt at the new state of things? Had Terry reckoned without his host? Might it be that she was not in love with her cousin, after all? For a moment these questions flashed through his mind, and set his heart to beating quickly. Then Terry's words about his uncle came back to him, and all these swiftly raised hopes fell to the ground. It was a recognized fact in the family. There could be no mistake. The girl was tired out, and probably not conscious of her own expression. His summer had been a failure, but it was not her fault; she had simply treated him as she would have treated any friend of her uncle's and Terry's, and he had made an egregious fool of himself — that was all. He went back into the house and seated himself in the chair by the bed, where Robin had been a few moments before.

CHAPTER XVI.

" Miss Cary, Terry is at the hotel, and would like to speak with you a moment."

Conrad delivered this message in a whisper, and held back the net door that Robin might pass out. They always spoke in whispers now, for Cy was so weak that even the ordinary tones of a friend's voice seemed to disturb him. He lay, for the most part, with closed eyes ; only opening them, at first eagerly, of late languidly, when the barrier-blinds were thrown open, morning and evening, and his gaze was free to wander away over the well-beloved woods and meadows without.

Robin's face was white, and her eyes heavy with watching and anxiety. She crossed the village street with a step very different from that of even a few days previous. Conrad's eyes followed her with a yearning pain in them. He would so gladly have shielded her from this trouble that was wearing her out, if he could! Yet he never sounded the trouble to half its real depth. How should he? He had, for her sake, put himself to the useless torture of a few, apparently casual, words with the parson since that morning when she had looked at him so strangely, and the parson had fully borne out Terry's assertion by his easy taking for granted of family plans. Conrad could do no more; he had laid that ghost of a glance; that was all he had gained. Somehow it never occurred to him that the parson's taking for granted might be a little *too* easy.

In the bare hotel parlor, darkened and close with its shut windows, Terry stood waiting. He had not seen his cousin for several days. He came forward eagerly to meet her, and looked earnestly into her face.

"Robin," he said, "you are killing yourself! you are not the same girl, at all, that you were when I came here, three weeks ago."

"No," she answered dreamily, "I am not the same girl that I was then."

"Robin, don't say such dreadful things!"

cried Terry, forgetting that he had said the same himself. Robin's tone made the words sound differently, somehow, and alarmed him. " You will grow foolish yourself if you hang over that boy day and night so. Come, you have manifested your affection for him quite enough ; let some one else step in now, and you come home with me. Uncle and I want you : the boy is all right."

Robin lifted her eyes to his face half wonderingly. "Terry," she said slowly, " the boy is dying. Did Uncle Ike not tell you ? "

" What do you mean ? Uncle said something about his being very weak; but of course he is weak. He will be all over that presently. Don't get rattled, Robin."

" Terry, *can't* you understand ? Cy has never got on as he should, and since Monday he has failed rapidly. Now, he is dying; Dr. Farnham says so."

Robin had not spoken with any thought of the effect her words might produce, but they struck home. She was surprised at the change that came over the young man's face. His was but an outer crust of selfishness, after all. Underneath, waiting only the right touch to develop it, lay the man's strong heart which ever beats quick response

to the appeal of helplessness and suffering.
Terry had really felt concerned for Cy, but
chose not to show it; to cover it up, indeed,
with an extra degree of careless indifference.
He had never dreamed but that the fat
boy would be all right again in due time,
"if only the women would not cosset him to
death." Now he could blind himself to the
real fact no longer, and back to his mind
came, vividly as if it had been but yester-
day, the scene in the woods at Porter's Pond.
He turned away and leaned against the mantel, his head resting on his folded arms.

Robin, who had kept aloof in the old
thoughtless, self-satisfied days, drew near
him now and laid one hand on his shoulder.

"Poor Terry!" she said softly.

"Oh, Robin," he cried, raising his head
again and looking her full in the face, "it
was not my fault! You don't think it was
my fault, do you?"

"No, you meant no harm; you were only
bent upon your own pleasure. But, oh,
Terry! I do believe a selfish man is the
cause of more misery in this world than even
a cruel one, sometimes."

"Am I a selfish man, Robin?"

"No, you are only a boy. A thoughtless,

careless boy. But oh, Terry!" she cried, again, "never let it grow upon you or you will break somebody's heart one day."

"Not yours! I will never break yours, Robin!" he exclaimed eagerly, all unconscious how thoroughly he had done his best to break it of late. "Don't you know that you can do anything with me? Don't you know that you are the only girl I ever cared a straw for? I have loved you all my life, I think. What a happy summer we might have had together, and to think of its being all upset! But we have September yet; we will make up for what is lost, won't we?" And, characteristically forgetting all his trouble of the moment before, he took the hand which had lain upon his shoulder, gently, in his own.

The girl drew it swiftly back, and herself up to her full queenly height.

"Cousin Terry, this is no time for idle words; but since you have spoken as you have I must needs answer, that you may *never* speak in such a way again!"

"Never! What can you possibly mean, Robin? Of course I shall speak. Of course you must know that I shall. A man can't keep quiet forever. I have waited two years to please Uncle Ike, but now I am free to please myself."

"You are too free, by far, to please me! Terry, I do not want to get angry to-day, even with you, but you make it very hard for me to help it. Once for all," she added, proudly, "if you have ever deceived yourself, or — or any one else, with the idea that I care for you in any way save as a cousin, let the deception be done away with at once, — at once! for I do not, and never can. You know I never can."

"I don't know anything of the sort! Why can't you? Why can't you?" he repeated, when she did not answer.

"Because — because it is impossible, that is all." Her pale face grew a shade paler, and the firm line of the lips deepened.

"It is not impossible, it cannot be impossible! unless" — and he seized her hand again, but not so gently this time, and held it in a tight grip.

"Let me go, Terry; I am needed. I must go back to Cy."

"Wait! Robin, tell me, do you —, by Jove! it's tough to have to ask the question for another fellow — do you care for any one else?"

"Let me go, Terry!" she cried, blushing furiously now over all her paleness, "you have no right to ask such a question; how *dare* you?" and she wrenched her hand indignantly away, and flung open the door which he had closed when she first came in.

He let her go then, and stood watching her as she went back. much faster than she had come, across the street and disappeared among the trees. Then he strode to the shed where old Nahum and the chaise were in waiting, sprang in, and drove off homeward.

"She did not deny it!" he said to himself, bitterly, paying small heed to his horse's movements. "Of course it's Faulkner. I did not think he would cut me out like this. Pshaw! what am I saying? he knew nothing of it, how should he? Con is not that kind of fellow. He would be much more likely to — By Jove!" Terry sat bolt upright as a sudden light flashed upon past and present. "Was *that* what he was gulping down under his hat the other day? Of course he loves her. How could he help it? and yet he shook hands with me and wished me well. Poor old Con! I reckon we 've upset one another's apple-carts about alike, after all. No we have n't, though," he added, tumbling back into the old bitterness and the chaise corner both at once, " for she loves him.   He does n't know it now, but he will. It won't hurt him to worry awhile ; he has n't got to suffer all his life, as I have."   And the poor fellow groaned, in honest anguish, at the terrible vista of empty years which he was, for the moment, convinced really lay spread before him.

Nahum, unused to groans, felt himself called upon to pause, and accordingly came to a sudden halt right where he stood, which happened to be half-way down a short, steep pitch, thereby bringing his grief - relaxed driver's nose into sharp communication with the dasher.

There could have been no more effective counter-irritant administered ; it was as good as a whiff of ammonia.   Terry picked himself up in a hurry and, pocketing his misery for a more convenient opportunity, proceeded to impel the old horse up-hill at the point of the whiplash, and the top of his climbing speed ; thereby arousing in his equine breast a mixture of amazement and mild indignation which expressed itself in frequent shakes of his wise old head, and layings back of his long, hairy ears ; the while his fat, respectable sides fairly heaved and creaked with the unprecedented exertion.

" Don't say one word, Uncle Ike ! " exclaimed Terry, the waters of Marah closing over him again as his uncle came out to hear the latest report from the cottage and glanced with astonishment at Nahum, hot and wheezy and turning one dumfoundered eye upon his master as who should say, " Behold ! "

" Don't say one word ! I 'm as wretched as thunder, and have been taking it out on the horse, that 's all. I 've made a confounded mess of everything ; and — and Cy 's dying, they tell me ! " and with a break in his voice at the last words, the poor young fellow sprang away upstairs to hide his sorrow and disappointment in his own room.

After all, in order to have much of the man in him at three and twenty, a boy must have considerable of the baby, too.

CHAPTER XVII.

CHRISTINA ROSSETTI.

"MISS ROBIN, will ye sing me somethin'?"

Robin was beside the western window, looking out into the sunset with absent eyes. She turned from her own thoughts instantly, at the sick boy's call, and went over to where he lay.

"Indeed I will, Cy. Do you care what?"

"That one they sing in church sometimes, 'baout brooks an' sunshine an' things, an' the feller that could n't stop more 'n over night."

So Robin sang the old hymn while Cy lay, drinking in the sweet words and tones, with closed eyes and a happy face.

"I 'm a pilgrim, and I 'm a stranger,
I can tarry, I can tarry but a night.
Do not detain me, for I am going
To where the streamlets are ever flowing."

Conrad, coming over at that moment from

his tea, withdrew his outstretched hand from
the tell - tale latch, and sat down in the
shadow without, to listen.

> "There the sunbeams are ever shining,
>   I am longing, I am longing for the sight !
>   Within a country unknown and dreary,
>   I have been wandering forlorn and weary."

" Poor Cy ! " thought the unseen listener,
while the tender voice sang through the refrain, " you will be neither forlorn nor weary
long, — your wanderings are almost over
now."

> " Of that country to which I 'm going
>   My Redeemer, my Redeemer is the light !
>   There is no sorrow, nor any sighing,
>   Nor any sickness, nor any dying.
>   I 'm a pilgrim, and I 'm a stranger ;
>   I can tarry, I can tarry, but a night. "

The girl's tones were inexpressibly sweet
and comforting as she sang the last lines, but
they did not tremble, nor falter.   Robin had
got beyond trembling ; her self-command was
something wonderful.   Cy's voice broke the
silence when she ceased.

" Miss Robin, is Mr. Jacks'n anywheres
raound naow ? "   Terry's name had never
passed his lips before, in conscious moments,
since the accident.

" Yes, Cy.   Would you like to see him ? "

The answer to this was inaudible, but apparently affirmative, for Robin presently came to the door and opened it. Certainly she had known nothing of Conrad's proximity, until he rose from the low seat by the door, and stood before her; yet she did not hesitate, nor seem surprised at seeing him there, but quietly desired him to send some one for Terry, and went back, herself, into the house. When he returned from doing her bidding she was singing again.

An hour went by. The moon was like transparent silver over the tops of the dark pines. One by one the stars pierced through the unclouded dome above like points of golden nails driven by an unseen hand. The shadows deepened and darkened as the heavenly brightness waxed — deepened and darkened in the sick-room as well, while the minutes winged their unremitting flight toward the supreme instant that should be, for him who lay and waited there, the swallowing up of every earthly shadow in the fullness of eternal light and joy.

Wheels rolled up the street, and stopped. Robin thought it would be Terry, but it was not. It was Dr. Farnham. He looked at Cy, felt his pulse, and then, thrusting one hand under the blanket, felt the extremities also. Then he walked to the window where Robin had been sitting, and looked out into the moonlight till Conrad, who had come into the room with him, began to think he would never speak. When he did, it was only to utter some remark upon the beauty of the night. Then he came back to his patient.

"Good night, Cy. I shall be in again in the morning."

The heavy lids lifted, and Cy smiled straight into the doctor's face. A smile of such intelligence, so full of a strange, unearthly peace, that the tender-hearted physician could not meet it. He was turning abruptly away when the boy held out his hand.

"Good-by, doctor; ye 've been dreadful good ter me."

The old man grasped the weak, white fingers almost convulsively in his own warm, muscular hand, and fairly broke down into a sudden sob. Then he hurried away. "Poor fellow!" he said to Conrad on the doorstep, "he 'll not live the night out. I 've an urgent case five miles off, or I should stay to see him through. He 'll do without me though; he won't suffer, probably. Poor Cy, poor Cy! if he 's a fool. I begin to think

the rest of us are all knaves!" and the kind
doctor wrung Conrad's hand hard, and drove
off to care for the little new life that was
nearing its beginning, while this one was
drawing to an end.

As Conrad turned to go in again, a hand
was laid upon him from behind. It was Terry's. He was very pale, and his lips were
tightly compressed.

" Poor fellow!" said his friend, " I am
sorry for you, but we could not help it;
he asked for you."

" Of course; you did quite right. Only
— I'd rather be shot myself than face him.
Shall I go in now?"

The sound of his voice brought Robin to
the door, and she remained outside while her
cousin went in alone. Within the little room
it was dusky. Terry, coming from the light
without, could see nothing at first.

" Mister Jacks'n — is that you?"

The feeble voice guided Terry's feet to
where its owner lay.

" Oh, Cy!" was all the young man could
say, while the determined lips began, in spite
of him, to tremble.

" Don't feel bad! I did n't send for ye ter
bother ye. I only thought I 'd kind er like ter

say good-by, an’ then — I wanted ter ask
a favor of ye.”

“ I never meant to hurt you, Cy.”

“ I know ye did n’t ; ’t was my fault, not
yourn. I had n’t no bisness ter grab the
pistil so, but ye see — that squir’l was an
old friend o’ mine, an’ I never had many
friends like smart folks, — so I could n’t
bear ter see him shot at. Likely he won’t
miss me so much as I should him.”

Terry was beyond speech by this time.
He could only register an inward vow that
no squirrel should ever come to grief at his
hands again. There fell a silence.

“ Mister Jacks’n.”

Terry made a tremendous effort. “ Yes,
Cy, I am here.”

“ Ye know I had a favor ter ask ye.”

“ Ask away, Cy. I ’ll do it, if it half
kills me ! ”

The fat boy scrutinized his face for a moment with eyes that, from being always
something veiled in expression, had come,
of late, to have in them a look of more than
earthly clearness.

“ Ye would n’t ha’ done it — oncet.” he
said slowly, “ but now, I kinder think ye
will.”

"What is it, Cy?"

"Mister Forkner an' Miss Robin — I can't say it good, but I guess ye know what I mean."

"Go on."

"There's somethin' gone wrong atween 'em. I can see it, ef I *be* a fool, an' I thought, mebbe — you could set it right ef ye wanted ter."

A sudden frown darkened the young man's brow, and his foot beat impatiently against the floor. Cy gazed up at him wistfully.

"He said ye was his friend. Miss Robin alwers said folks oughter be willin' ter do anythin' fer their friends."

No answer. Cy's auditor had hitched himself half round in his chair, and was drumming on the back of it with his fingers. Doubtless he would have liked to bolt, but invisible bands held him fast. "Greater love hath no man than this, that a man lay down his life for his friend." The divine declaration, called back to him by means of dying human lips, was ringing in judgment through heart and brain. Much as he loved his cousin, hard as his trouble was to bear, something told him, even then, that Conrad's love was the truer, and nobler, and more deserving. He had always pleased himself till now; could he find it in him to so far rise above all his former life as to set himself aside, and, with his own hand, as it were, make the way clear for his friend? Cy's voice broke in again.

" Ye like *her*, don't ye? I alwers thought ye liked her dreadful well."

" I always thought so too," muttered Terry to himself, " but I'm beginning to think I must have liked myself a darned sight better ! "

" I can't hear ye ; did ye say ye 'd do it ? " asked the boy eagerly, though his voice was fast becoming weaker.

Poor Terry! he sprang from his chair and sought the window, as the doctor had done. There was a mighty warfare waging within him. Love for Robin and innate selfishness arrayed themselves over against friendship and honor, and the fight was fierce. Standing there in the evening hush, broken only by the quick breathing of the dying boy, while the moon stole gradually further and further south until one bright beam fell athwart the darkness of the silent room, the young man fought, in a brief ten minutes, the decisive battle of his life.

He won it. Won with it also a strength and calmness that had not been his before. He went back to where Cy lay, watching him with anxious eyes, and bending over the low bed said, quietly, —

"So far as it lies in my power, Cy, I will do what you ask."

The boy's look of gratitude was good to see.

"I thought ye would," he said.

"What else can I do?"

"Nothin', there ain't nothin' else. Only, don't never worry 'cause I — did n't git well. It 's all right, I guess."

Another silence. Then Cy once more held out his hand.

"Good-by."

But Terry could not say good-by. He could only hold the passive hand a moment longer, and lay it gently down, and go away.

"One moment, Mr. Faulkner, if you please! Janet has gone to Cy; he will not miss us for a little. I wish to ask you a question."

Robin turned from watching Terry, as he walked quickly away, and detained Conrad with these words. Her manner was

very quiet, and unhurried. This was no
sudden impulse, it was the outcome of a
determination slowly taken, and therefore
strong. She would not give up her friend
without one last effort. He alone could
offer an explanation of the state of things
existing between them, and since he did
not do so, she would ask it. Then at least
she might feel that no false pride of hers
had barred the way.

"Do you remember a promise that we
made one Sunday, soon after you came to
Ockley?"

Conrad's heart bounded — and stood still;
but his reply, after a moment, came firm
and low.

"Perfectly."

"Have you kept it?"

"Miss Robin," with the old memory the
old name came, unawares, to his lips, "it
has become impossible for me to keep that
promise; I must ask you to release me from
it."

He was not looking at her; but far away
at the river, shining and writhing in the
moonlight like a silver serpent. He did
not see the look of intensest pain and disappointment that held her face for an instant,

whitening it to the very lips. When at last she spoke, the chill of the clear September evening was in her still, proud voice.

"You are released, Mr. Faulkner. Shall we go in?"

Nine! — ten! — eleven! — twelve!

The hours rang slowly out, one after another, from the church tower close by. They were the only sounds that broke the stillness of that long, hard night. In the feeble light of the little night-lamp sat the three watchers — silent.

Cy's eyes were closed, his breathing quiet. They thought him sleeping, and feared to break that slumber by a word.

One! — two! — three!

The early morning air grew chill. Robin stepped lightly across the floor, and fetching her shawl wrapped it carefully about the shoulders of her old nurse. The poor woman, well-nigh sick herself from constant watching and grief, lay back, half dozing, in her chair beside her grandson. The other two, with only the width of the narrow room between them as they sat, yet separated in truth by a distance greater than miles could measure — greater even than that viewless space which death itself interposes between loving hearts — felt no drowsiness, felt no cold. Their thoughts, continually passing and repassing, wrapped them in numb bitterness as in a mantle, which the hours, as they sped unheeded by, but gathered the more closely, fold on fold.

Four!

How loud and solemn the separate strokes fell upon their ears! Conrad involuntarily shuddered; it seemed as if the old clock were tolling a death-knell.

There came another sound along the village street; faint in the distance, growing more and more distinct as it neared and passed the house, and dying gradually away as it had come. The sharp, clicking sound of a horse's trotting feet. Dr. Farnham was coming back from his night's work; he would be in again presently.

The slender, clean-cut sound seemed to rouse the dulled sense of hearing as the broader, accustomed voice of the bell had failed to do. Cy stirred a little, and opened his eyes.

" Gran'mer ! "

The old lady started from her doze, gave one keen glance into her grandson's face, and, dropping to her knees beside him, buried her gray head in the pillow.

" Mister Forkner — Miss Rob " —

They were beside him in an instant. One look of loving gratitude and farewell to Conrad, then he turned to Robin. He tried to speak, but life and strength were fast slipping from him, and the words were indistinguishable. The rapidly glazing eyes looked into hers the supplication he could not utter, and, translating that look by the power of her own loving heart, the girl bent gently down and pressed her soft, warm lips upon his death-cold forehead.

For one brief instant the boy's face was transfigured! Then the glad light died, slowly, from his eyes, the pale lips set themselves in that last, loving smile ; the breath came slowly, — slowly, — fluttered, — and was gone! And something which seemed to be Cy, yet was not, lay peaceful, still, upon the little bed, while the sunrise of a golden autumn day was flushing in the east.

Cy had passed out from under the shadows, forever, into the glad high-light of Heaven's eternal joy.

CHAPTER XVIII.

Song.

Cy died on Friday, and on Sunday they buried him. The little church was full to overflowing, for the fat boy, with his simple, unselfish ways and quiet life, had won for himself, even among those who had laughed loudest at his oddities, more friends than he had ever dreamed of. If there were some, among the people gathered there, who came merely from motives of curiosity, it mattered little ; for even they read something, in the still sweetness of that peaceful face, which touched a very tender chord, and made them too, for the moment, friends.

But Cy could not be called " the fat boy" any longer. His sickness had been so far kind that it had pruned away much of the outward, physical deformity which had hidden his real self like a mask ; and there was revealed in death something of the delicate outline of face and feature that he came into the world with. The child made manifest again after twenty years of blighted, and overgrown, and, by the world's standard, useless existence. And yet, there was more also. The child had become a man.

CYRUS BURNS.
Aged 25 years.

Coffin-plates do not lie. The clear-cut silver lettering was there to speak to-day, with silent authority the fact that, unperceived and unrecognized, a man had been growing up among them, all these years, where careless eyes had descried but an overgrown, half-witted boy. "The eyes of the Lord run to and fro throughout the whole earth, to show himself strong in the behalf of them whose heart is perfect toward Him." Through the darkness, as of old, God's hand had been at work all these years creating a soul for his kingdom. That kingdom which, however great, however wise, no man can ever hope to enter except he first lay aside all mere outward seeming and become " as a little child."

Terry had begged, as the only thing he could do, to be allowed to provide the flowers ; and the simple casket was fairly hidden from view beneath roses, and ferns, and heliotropes, and fair, white, stainless lilies. Their rich fragrance rose up, like incense, through the stillness, and mingled itself with the sweet organ notes that floated down to meet it; the bright September sunshine and the soft September air flowed in, through open windows, unreproved; late lingering birds that had sung their exultant love-songs for Cy's listening ear in June, sang, all unconsciously, his requiem now; while a great golden butterfly, attracted by the bloom and perfume, fluttered in over the heads of those assembled there, and hovered, like a radiant, risen soul above the delicate blossoms and the sleeping form they covered.

"The wisdom of this world is foolishness with God."

People said " the parson fair outdid himself " in the solemn, touching, beautiful discourse he delivered from these wonderful words. He himself, looking down from his pulpit upon the quiet face below, remembering words and smiles that had moved those still lips, from time to time, through weeks of suffering bravely borne, felt to the very bottom of his heart, that simple Cy had outdone them all.

Hard as that hour was for all in the little band of friends that had been nearest to the boy: for his grandmother, sitting there alone in her old age; for Conrad, with his bright, brief summer-time behind him, his darkened life before; for Robin, suffering in outward silence, pouring forth her heart's trouble only in the quivering, throbbing organ-tones that had been born of like anguish centuries before her day; it was hardest, by far, for Terry. His had been the hand to weave all this intricacy of grief, and pain, and misunderstanding into the bright, happy web of his friends' living; his the deed and word that had transformed their cloudless sunshine into the shadow of death itself. And to undo the mischief in such incomplete wise as was left possible to him, he must rend asunder forever the airy fabric of his own hopes, which, for two long years, he had been so blithely fashioning; must lay upon his life-canvas, side by side with the brightest vision of his three-and-twenty years, the deep, dark shadows of repentance and renunciation.

It was agreed, on all sides, that if the parson had never preached, Miss Robin had never played, "anything like so feelin' afore."

It is absurd for people to assert that any given musical composition has its own invariable tale to tell. There were at least two hearts in the little church that day for which those clinging minor chords bore hidden meaning; yet the message that came to the one was totally unlike that which the other received.

When all was over; when the flower-laden casket had been lowered to its resting-place in the spot Cy had himself chosen by the river-boundary of the little village cemetery; when all the people had gone away, and the cool, green sods had been carefully replaced above the new - made mound, Conrad and Robin, standing one on either side, raised their heads as by mutual consent, and, looking full into one another's face, clasped hands across the grave.

"Shall we say good-by, here? it is a good place." Conrad's voice was low, and not quite steady, but Robin's clear tone never wavered as she answered him.

"The very best. Good-by!"

Without another word, another look, they parted, and went their separate ways. He to the hotel to pack his trunk, and be driven a little later to the Falls, thence to take the midnight train for Boston. She to the side-gate of the cemetery, where Terry and her uncle were already waiting.

" Robin, my dear, I have a call in another direction. Abel Rogers has had a second stroke. Terry will drive you home. I must hunt up Conrad again, too, and say good-by to him. The poor boy seems sadly cut up by all that has happened. We must get him here again, another year, for a better ending to his visit. Go right to bed, dear child," he added, putting her carefully into the chaise, " you need rest, sadly. Terry will excuse you. I shall be back to tea."

Rest, or something, Robin did indeed need sadly ; but the strain had been too intense and long-continued for relaxation to come at once. Bolt upright, white, and silent she sat by Terry's side, while Nahum, remembering his former experience with his present driver, bestirred himself to climb the hills alertly.

CHAPTER XIX.

Christina Rossetti.

From time to time Terry glanced at his cousin, but her eyes never once turned toward him. There was a fixed, battle-worn, enduring look in her face that he could not bear to see, and yet that he could scarce keep from noting, stealthily, either. A deep, long sigh of relief fled from the girl's pale lips when Nahum came at last to his deliberate stop before the home doorway ; and she sprang from the chaise, and passed swiftly through the hall, as one who seeks to escape and would not be stopped.

Terry understood, yet he stopped her, just this once. He overtook her at the stairfoot, and laid a gentle, but detaining hand upon her own as it rested on the rail.

" Cousin Robin," he said, quietly, calling her, with a generous grace that was something new in Terry, by the name he had never used before since they were boy and girl, " I am going back to New York to-night; won't you say good-by ? "

" *You*, Terry ? "

Her voice spoke mingled surprise and re-lief, and the little emphasis on one word told of another feeling, too. She had not forgot-ten that some one else was to take the mid-night train.

" Yes, *I*," replied her cousin, with a little accentuation on his part. He knew so well that there would probably be but one pas-senger from Ockley, after all.

" I have not said good-by to uncle, — I could n't; you must do that for me."

Then, seeing him so brave and unself-ish, so much a man in his disappointment, Robin's heart smote her. She came down the step or two which she had mounted, and held out both hands to him.

" Terry, if I have seemed hard and un-feeling, forgive me ! I am both, I believe, just now. It seems, somehow, as if I were frozen up." The dreary little smile upon her tired face touched him to the quick. He had been forbidden to feel for himself, he was beginning to feel for others.

" Don't speak like that, Robin ! " he exclaimed, drawing a quick, sharp breath, " it hurts. I know I have done a horrible two weeks' work, but it can be undone, some of it, and it shall." And the young fellow drew himself up with a look of resolution on his face that had never been there before.

Robin did not understand. She thought he spoke of himself, and his own troubles; she was glad for him that he could speak so bravely. " That is right, Terry ; undo it all, undo it quickly. It was never meant to be, or I should have wanted it too, and I do not. The right one is ready for you, some- where, and you are ready for her, or will be. You mistook one girl for another, that was all."

" I don't know that. It may be so, but I am not quite ready to agree with you now. If there be another Robin in the world I have yet to find her, and " — Terry lifted his head proudly — " anything less I do not want ! "

" You are a noble fellow, Terry ! I never knew half how noble before. You will find a great deal more, some day, than you ever found in me ; and meanwhile, I am proud to be your — cousin."

She would not call him " friend ; " that

word had been profaned. She held out her hand, both hands, again. He took them in his own and looked, with a long, wistful, hungry look, into her eyes.

"Good-by, little girl," he said, tenderly; "if only one of us can be happy, I am glad that one is you." Then, all at once, while she looked wonderingly at him, he caught her in his arms, kissed her once, twice, three times, turned, and was gone.

She went slowly on, upstairs, wondering still at his strange last words, and feeling that in uttering this third farewell, she had also bidden good-by to all her happy girl-hood, forever.

As for Terry, now that the supreme moment was over, all his new-found strength seemed to desert him. It had been comparatively easy to speak brave, unselfish words with Robin's hand in his, and Robin's eyes looking approval at him: but now he had left her behind, and the hardest part of his task lay yet before him. He plunged down the steep bank to the river, and strode along the narrow path that hugged the winding stream. It was a weary, dreary way to his unwilling feet. Every tree, every rock, every clump of ferns and tuft of water-weeds that he had known so long and well, had a word for him that day. The happy summer-time was over and gone forever. Autumn had already begun to lay her withering finger on many a leaf and flower. "The time of the singing of birds" was past; only here and there a stray partridge crept shyly away through the undergrowth, or rose with hurrying whirr from some hidden covert at his feet. The river flowed on still. Summer or winter its ceaseless waters never failed nor faltered; yet even the river bore a sadness in its song that had not been there before. The cardinal flowers were all gone; they had picked the bright scarlet spikes together, Robin and Conrad, and Cy and he, only a month ago. Now the month was gone, and the flowers: and of those who sought their vivid blooms so gayly two were drifting apart who should have been together; and one had passed away from birds, and flowers, and friends, out of hearing of the rapid rippling river, that, flowing ever on amid his old-time haunts, flowed also now beside his still, green grave; and one was leaving far behind the Eden of his boyhood to forge out, with God's help, upon the world's rough anvil that "whole armor" for the want of which so many a gallant head has been laid low in the first charge on life's fierce battle-field. The true metal for it all was in him; the hammer and the anvil would not fail; but first must come the fiery furnace, and the purging, and Terry shivered before the fierce, hot pain even while he went his swift, unswerving way to meet it.

In the stuffy hotel bedroom Conrad was packing his trunk. Clothing, books, and papers lay on the floor about him; in his hand was the manuscript of his partly written story. He had risen to his feet and stood turning over the leaves with a grave face, as Terry came in. The afternoon had been cool, and in the little open grate lay the smouldering remains of a recent fire. Terry flung himself into a chair; something in the coincidence of things carried them both back, in memory, to the little New York study, and their last morning together there. They had been fast friends, these two.

"Nearly packed?" asked Terry, carelessly.

"All, but. I want to get rid of some of this — rubbish!" and hastily gathering up all the odds and ends of wrapping paper that lay scattered about Conrad thrust them into the grate, adding thereto the few sticks yet remaining in the wood-box. Then, taking several sheets from the pile of manuscript, he deliberately tore them across, and flung the fragments upon the blazing pile.

"Hold hard, Con!" exclaimed Terry, jumping up as the other was about to repeat the process, "what are you about?"

"Don't get excited, Terry; I am merely burning my ships — nothing more."

The words were light, but there was a bitter tone to them that his friend had never heard from him before.

"Don't do that, Con; you will want them again." And Terry coolly removed the pile of manuscript to a place of safety.

"Hardly. Just hand the stuff back here, please!"

But instead of doing as he was bid Terry came closer, and laid a hand on his friend's shoulder.

"Con, old man," he said, trying to smile and failing dismally, "don't get mad with a fellow. I'm going to say good-by in a few minutes, and you won't see me again, very soon. But first — you 're better up in history than I am — would what 's-his-name have burned his ships if there had n't been hard fighting to be done, in a strange land?"

Conrad looked up in surprise; it was a new freak for Jackson to be putting history questions.

"What do you mean?" he said; "my papers, please! I 'm in rather a hurry."

But Terry had thrust his hands into his pockets, and was striding up and down the room; letting off steam according to his old habit.

"I mean — just that;" he answered, slowly, as if he found his words hard to speak. "You 're making ready for hard fighting, and there 's no fighting to be done. Or if there is, it 's not for you. You can go back to — wherever you came from!"

Conrad stood stock-still, arrested midway in his progress across the room, his face becoming like marble for whiteness and fixity. "Do you know what you are saying, boy?" he cried, hoarsely and low; "if you don't, for Heaven's sake quit talking! if you do, speak out — speak plainly."

Poor Terry! his sharp hour had come. There was a hard, dull pain at his heart, but the man was in him, he never flinched.

"Con," he answered, turning, like an animal at bay, to face his death - blow, "I know just two things, for sure. Robin does

not love me, and never will ; and she does
— and will always — love some one else.
Who that some one is you know best, I
think."

He had fought bravely, but he could fight
no more. The strength had gone clean out
of him with those few, plain words. He
turned to the darkening window and laid
his vanquished head down, wearily, upon his
folded arms.

Victory, too, is hard to bear sometimes.
The swift, triumphant gladness which had
flashed into Conrad's eyes at Terry's words
faded and died away as he noted the price
at which his triumph had been bought.
Thankfulness and joy were there still, but
they shone through something very like
tears. There was silence, for a time, between the two.

Then Conrad crossed the room and laid
his arm, lightly, across his friend's shoulders.

"Terry," said he, "I little thought, three
months ago, that you and I would ever
come to stand on opposite sides of a thing
like this. It is useless to play the hypocrite,
now, and say I 'm sorry, for I 'm not. I 'm
glad !" (the ring in his voice told how glad.)
" But I have n't suffered these weeks past to

crow over you now, and a man who can do
what you have done is not to be pitied, exactly. There 's only one thing to be said.
When I thought things were in your favor,
hard as it was, I never grudged you your
happiness for a moment. I know you well
enough to feel sure that you will never
grudge me mine. Our friendship can stand
even this strain."

" Yes, by Jove, it can ! " exclaimed Terry,
raising his head proudly, but keeping his
face carefully turned toward the window.
" I 'm hard hit, Con, and no mistake, but
I 'm not such a fool as to want what does n't
belong to me for all that. May be, some
day, as Robin said, I shall find what *does*
belong to me, and then — I 'll hold on in
spite of the devil ! " He grasped Conrad's
proffered hand in his own, appreciating for
the first time what that other hand-shake,
three weeks before, had cost his friend ; but
for all his brave words, the boy was sore at
heart ; and when Conrad had left the room,
he threw himself, face downward, upon the
low lounge by the fire and lay there, motionless and still, while the red flame danced
and flickered — casting weird shadows over
walls and ceiling, and rose, and fell, and

sobbed itself to death in a blue quiver. The embers glowed, and deadened, and cooled to soft, white ashes; but yet the prostrate figure lay there and did not stir.

CHAPTER XX.

" Thou, and the evening star, and she and I."
                                        EDWIN ARNOLD.

CONRAD went on and up, over the hills, in the cool, early evening. On and up till the narrow brown road lay in a long, curling ribbon behind him, and only the last steep hill remained to climb. He had never thought to climb that hill again!

He had come fast, for his feet kept pace with his brain, and his brain was in a whirl. He had not paused, as yet, to look back over the past. Possibly, had he done so, the future might have seemed a bit dubious to him, remembering Robin's proud, still face of late. He had not got so far, either, as to hazard a peep at the future, or, possibly, that might have sent him about-face to the past for counsel. He had thought and action for the present only, but such thought and action were at high pressure.

The fair full moon was rising in silent majesty over the eastern hills ; the shadows

of the tree-trunks along the roadside fell
like black, forbidding bars across his way.
He trod them under foot, and pressed on.
Far off in the woods an owl was hooting;
the cool autumn wind stirred fitfully among
the branches, and over in the meadow count-
less fall crickets polished their black legs
with busy chirping. He opened the little
side - gate, noiselessly, and let himself
through. It seemed a lifetime, almost,
since he had last laid his hand upon its
iron latchet. No one was in the porch, no
one in the study. He passed out again, and
round to the side door-yard. Mrs. Bloom
was coming across from the barn-yard with
a milk pail in either hand: the moonbeams
flashing back from their shiny tin curves as
she walked.

"Is that you, Parson Cary?" she called
out, catching sight of a man's tall figure
emerging from the house shadow; "we're
late with the milkin' ter-night, 'caount o'
the funer'l puttin' us back some."

"It's I, Mrs. Bloom. Where is — everybody?"

"The Lord preserve us all!" ejaculated
the housekeeper, letting fall her milk-pails
where she stood, and coming forward quick-

ly. "Where is everybody, sure enough? Or where *hev* they be'n, ruther! I never dreamp' o' seein' *your* face ag'in, Mister Forkner. Be ye come ter stop this time?" she scrutinized him sharply as she spoke.

"That is not for me to say," replied Conrad, gravely.

"H'm! donno as 't is — naow. Three weeks back I sh'd ha' said 't was — in a maysure."

"Where is Miss Robin?" asked Conrad, again, chafing inwardly at being so far dependent upon the housekeeper's clemency that he must stay where he was till she chose to answer him.

Mrs. Bloom's rigid features relaxed, and there came a tearful pucker into her fat face that would have been ludicrous but for its cause.

"She's in trouble, poor thing, that's where she is; an' I wish all the fellers in York had be'n drownded in a pint pot afore she'd had her pretty, happy life destroyed by 'em! As ef 't warnt enough ter see poor Cy a-layin' dead there to-day, all along o' that kerless Terry an' his murderin' blunderbuss; but Miss Robin must be goin' round with somethin' in her lovin' little

heart that's worse 'n any bullit, fer it's turn-
in' her cold an' still too, only she can't die
an' git threw with it like Cy's done. She
come out here, just now, with her white face,
an' cold hands, an' her big eyes fit ter burn
us all up; an' not a word ter me nor nobody, but up an' away through the cold, wet
grass, with her thin shoes an' not a rag over
her shoulders, poor dear, an' I not darin' ter
speak a word, like an old fool!" She put
her apron furtively to her eyes, and Conrad
stood waiting. "Fer the Lord's sake, Mister Forkner," she exclaimed, facing round
upon him abruptly and fiercely, "ef ye've
found out what a durn' fool ye've be'n, an'
mean ter own to 't, go after her! She's in
the hill orchard."

Conrad waited for nothing further; he
had got all he asked for and a good deal
more. He hastened away, through the trees
and up the slope, the echoes of Mrs. Bloom's
unminced remarks yet buzzing in his ears
like a swarm of hornets; while she, worthy
woman, resuming the burden she had dropped
to battle so fearlessly in her young lady's behalf, followed him with damp eyes till he was
out of sight.

"Drat the men!" she said to herself,

as she hurried into the house and began
to bustle about to make up for lost time;
"they're queer critters, the best on 'em. *I*
know 'em! Some on 'em won't take no fer
an answer ef ye hit 'em over the head with
the shovel, an' more don't know beans when
they're right afore their noses! Ef ever I
see the course o' true love a-runnin' smooth
an' easy 't was this time, till that boy Terry
come pokin' around an' layin' hisself right
acrosst the stream like a dam — well never
mind; he ain't wuth swearin' about, an' he's
got a blamed good duckin' by it too, poor feller! that's one comfort."

Mrs. Bloom's remarks, like her sympa-
thies, were getting to be a good deal mixed.

Conrad passed up through the hill orchard; now in moonlight, now in shadow,
till, at the very top, from beneath spreading
apple-boughs that made a fragrant gloom,
he emerged into open pasture-space flooded
with silver light. At any other time the
clear, pure beauty of the night itself would
have held him spell-bound. A wonderful
shadow-play was going on all over the surrounding hill-sides, and down in the valley
below. But to-night he had eyes for only
one object in all the gracious panorama that

unrolled itself before him.　Robin, her white dress gleaming in the moonlight, stood by the old stone wall alone.　She did not hear him coming; her eyes were upon the far, immovable hills, and something of their uplifted strength was in the firm, true poise of her graceful figure, and the still set of her features, outlined against the light.　The girl was a soldier every inch.　She might suffer, or die, but it would be " on the field of battle," her face to the enemy's lines.

" Miss Robin ! "

He could feel, standing beside her, that she started from head to foot; but she turned instantly, unhesitatingly, and confronted him without a word.　Then he saw in her face the look of which Mrs. Bloom had spoken; the intense, wide-eyed look of one who has suffered beyond the possible relief of tears.　That look, without a spoken word, revealed at last, to his short-sightedness, all that she had been enduring through these hard days and nights when he had fancied he was having all the suffering to himself.　In the light of those dark, sorrowful eyes he stood convicted.

There was nothing for her to say; she had already done her utmost.　She stood and waited for him to speak.

He could be brave, as well as she. He looked her full in the face; the words came hardly, but they came for all that.

"I have been — mistaken. Three weeks ago something was told to me that blotted the very sunlight out of heaven itself. It was a mistake; but I believed it. I thought I had good reason to believe it. Now I see that I was wrong. Will you forgive me?"

"Who told you — something?"

Her words were clear and cold as if carved in ice, but the hard look in her eyes began to soften.

"Terry, himself." His words were clear too, but they were not cold, and his handsome face was all aglow.

"And who has told you differently now?"

"Terry, himself."

"Brave boy!" Her eyes shone, and a soft color crept up into her cheeks.

"Brave, yes, he is all that! Not one man in ten thousand would have spoken as he spoke to-night. His words made me glad; they lifted a weight from my heart that had gone nigh to crushing it. But what is it all to profit me unless — you forgive me, Robin?"

She drew herself up to her full height,

and the glorious rush of color to cheeks and brow was something to see as she answered him in impetuous words.

"Mr. Faulkner, what the past has been to us, we both know too well for either to attempt denial. It has been much, very much to me; I am not ashamed to own it!" Truly there was no shame, nor need for it, in the deep, womanly eyes that met his so steadfastly. She went on, more hurriedly: "When I saw, as I could not help seeing, that something had gone wrong, I was sorry — I was hurt, but that was all. I felt so sure you would make it all plain, so sure," the steady voice wavered a little here, "you would keep your promise as I kept mine. For I have kept it!" she asserted proudly, "kept it in the face of much that would have seemed, to many an older woman than I, excuse sufficient for breaking it. Kept it to the extent of reminding you of your own, and you — flung back the friendship you were first to seek!"

The pain and bitterness of that last night at the cottage were in her face once more as they had been then; and Conrad's eyes were not upon the river this time, he saw it all.

"I was a fool!" he cried, hotly, " a

blind, blundering, half-crazy fool! but I have suffered for it too. Can you forgive, Robin?"

She laid her right hand instantly into his, held out to take it.

" Yes, I can forgive."

" And forget?"

She would have withdrawn her hand, but he held it fast, as one who had no mind to let it go again.

" And forget, Robin?" he repeated, looking down into her face with earnest eyes.

" It's ill patching a broken friendship," she said slowly, but her voice had lost its clear control, and her eyes fell before his steady gaze.

He answered not a word, but the strong hand clasping hers drew her closer, closer, while the other arm crept round, unseen, and held her fast.

" Robin," he said, then, and the deep, full tones had a thrill in them that fell like music on her tired ears, " our friendship broke, not because it was weak, but because we tried to make it hold too much. There is another word, not half as long; but it contains all friendship and infinitely more besides. I think it is the word we have been spelling to ourselves all along. Shall we spell it together now?"

How should she answer when her heart was full, almost to bursting, with the meeting tides of sorrow and great joy? Not one word came from the firm-set lips; but they quivered away from their firmness, like a child's. She could do no more. The long, brave fight was ended; the fountains of the great deep were broken up; the proud little head drooped down, down, like a tired bird, to its resting - place, and Robin cried as though her heart would break.

A few days later old Ben Thacher and his sister Constance were sitting out under the trees on the lawn at Winford. That is, their bodies were there; where they themselves were is not so easy to say, for Mr. Thacher was sound asleep in his lounging-chair, and Miss Constance was deep in a book. For a long time the stillness remained unbroken, save as the wind rustled the leaves of the elm-branches overhead, or as the lady turned those of the volume in her hand. Suddenly there broke upon the stillness the ringing, metallic hoot of a locomotive whistle! Miss Constance dropped her book, consulted her watch, and poked her brother.

" Ben — Ben ! the train is at the junction ;
I heard it just now."

" My gracious, Constance ! what possessed
you to let me sleep so long ? Do my best, I
can't get to the station before he does, now."

" May be you will have time ; they wait at
the crossing, you know."

" Well, well, I must be off ! Hope Quinn
has got the horses in.   Will you come ? "

" No. I won't hinder you any more."

And indeed he did not give her a chance,
for he was halfway to the stables before the
words were well out of her mouth.

She laughed to herself as the buggy tore
down the road in a cloud of dust, and she
caught sight of her brother's hat lying on the
grass where he had tossed it before going to
sleep. Then she settled once more to her
reading, to be shortly roused, for the second
time, by a hand laid on her shoulder, and
Conrad Faulkner's pleasant voice in her ears.

When Mr. Thacher returned, ten minutes
later, hatless and crestfallen, without the
guest he went to seek, he found his sister
just where he had left her, but her face was
radiant, and the interrupted novel lay, in an
ignominious sprawl, upon the grass beside
the hat.

"Ho-ho, how self-satisfied we look, to be sure! Guess the conquering hero has arrove, after all. Did he drop from the clouds? and has he gone back the way he came?"

"Not a bit of it! He has only gone to his room. He got off at the crossing and cut through the woods."

"Cut me too, the rascal! However, I suppose this is no time for showing spite. Cupid's blind, he'd never see it if I did. How does the fellow look?"

"Well, and *very* happy, Ben."

"H'm! I suppose so; they all do — at first. Is he prepared to look happy till October for our exclusive benefit?"

"He wants us to give up the Moosehead plan, and go back to Oekley with him."

"I'll warrant he does, young scamp!" exclaimed the lawyer, with a beaming face; "after keeping us waiting all this time. You nipped that proposition in the bud, of course?"

"I said we would go."

"The deuce you did! You and he together make a pretty go-ahead team, old lady. There seems to be nothing left for me but to put my tail between my legs and trot along after the wagon. Hulloa! here's the fellow now!

Well, sir," seizing Conrad's two hands and working them briskly up and down like steam pumps, "I don't see as there's much left for me to say. Connie, here, seems to have said everything — and a little more. What train do we expect to take to-morrow morning? I must be packing up."

"Day after to-morrow will do very well," said Conrad, from whose happy face the gathered gravity of years was swept away.

" ' Do very well?' no such thing! I'll tell her you said so, though. 'Twas for your pleasure (and the old lady's) you came here; you shall go back for mine. If I can't boss the line of travel, at least I'll boss the time of starting. I want to see this girl with a bird's name that's been setting us all by the ears for three months, and upsetting all my plans. I want to inspect her dairy, and taste her butter, and find out whether or no she's fit to be a poor man's wife. For you're a poor man, you know, Con!" And Mr. Thacher bestowed a most undignified and vigorous wink upon his sister, in return for her remonstrant shake of the head.

" I know I used to think so," replied Conrad, not at all cast down; " I do not think so now."

" *Now*, — *now*, of course not! " repeated
the lawyer, trying in vain to frown. " Now's
a great time with you ; the heyday of youth,
and all that. But," he added abruptly, turning upon Conrad with a sharp scrutiny, " by
and by is coming, too. There are all sorts
of days in life, boy, as well as sunny ones.
Three months ago you said you could n't afford to keep a wife ; why have you changed
your mind ? "

And Conrad, looking straight into the old
man's face, answered, with all his great joy
shining in his eyes : —

" Because I cannot afford to live without her any longer."

When Robin carried the good news to Janet, the old woman's face fairly shone.

"Then a' 's come right at last, Miss Robin,
an' it 's I that 's main glad for ye baith ! If
ever onybody deserved the best things o' this
weary warl', it 's just them that 's gettin' 'em
noo."

" If only we could all be happy together ! "
said Robin, the one little cloud in all her
bright new sky coming over her face. as she
remembered through what depth of sorrow
this joy had been brought about.

“ An’ so we can,” replied Janet, cheerily;
“ wha ’s to hinder ? ”

“ When I think of Terry — and Cy ” —

“ Hoots, lassie ! ” interrupted her old nurse.
“ Ye ’ve no call to pity Maister Terry, my
dear. The lad’s pains are just wha’ folks ca’
‘ growin’ pains ; ’ he ’ll but be the bigger
mon for them, some day. An’ as for Cy —
my Cy,” added the old woman, with a tender gleam in her deep-set eyes, “ he ’s won
till the heart o’ it all. He would na’ change
places wi’ ony o’ ye ! ”

Robin’s face cleared, and the happy look
crept back again.

“ I min’ Maister Faulkner sayin’ one
day,” went on Janet, “ how we nane o’ us
ken muckle o’ ane anither’s shadows ; but
there ’s twa sides to that, as there maun be to
everything sae long ’s there ’s a hither an’ a
yon. Look at thae twa bonnie cloodies,”
pointing to where, at either side of the blue
dome above them, swam a soft-piled vapor
bank ; “ what for, suppose ye, the ane ’s
white as the driven snaw, an’ the ither black
as deith itsel’ ? ”

“ Because we are on the sunny side of one,
and the shady side of the other,” said Robin,
smiling.

“Aweel, apply that noo, as the pairson says, to life an’ deith, joy an’ sorrow ; aye remmemberin’ where we stan’. Aye rememberin’ too, that whan we win to the Lord’s stan’-point, we shanna see things one-sided ony mair. ‘The darkness an’ the licht are baith alike to Him ! ’ ”